State of the Heart

Carol Patterson

State of the Heart
and other stories

State of the Heart and other stories
ISBN 978 1 76041 760 4
Copyright © text Carol Patterson 2019
Cover painting: Doreen Locher

First published 2019 by
Ginninderra Press
PO Box 3461 Port Adelaide 5015
www.ginninderrapress.com.au

Contents

State of the Heart

The phone call came at seven in the morning. Tessa thrust a hand from her doona and reached for it.

'Joe's rung. He's ill.' It was George, her ex-husband, talking about their twenty-two-year-old son.

'Ill? What's wrong with him?'

'Didn't specify.'

'God, George, didn't you ask him?' She was fully awake now.

'Can you get up there? You're on holidays, aren't you?'

'To Jacky's Marsh!'

'He'll want you.'

'He rang you.'

'You can drive me up, then.' Not that she didn't want to go to her son, but there was a point to be made.

Tessa hung up before he could protest further and lay back against her pillows. So Joe was sick, again. She remembered when he'd hitched home from Sydney last year. He'd been staying with his uncle, her brother Tom, in Glebe, working out what he was going to do with his life. So much for that.

Sorting through the dirty clothes in his pack, she'd found a bill from the Big Ben Medical Centre, and a repeat prescription for antidepressants, and a folded summary of admission to the Royal North Shore Hospital. Her heart in her mouth, she'd skipped down to Final Diagnosis, and read 'acute asthma. ?intercurrent viral URTI'. He'd responded rapidly to nebulised ventolin, the notes said. No risk to his heart. His heart? She read up on it. An acute asthma attack can stress the heart, resulting in heart problems and, in extreme cases, a heart attack.

'I'm okay!' he'd shouted, when she'd confronted him.

With every gloomy look, she'd worried that he was depressed; with every cough, that he was asthmatic. Next thing, he'd gone to Jacky's Marsh, squatting in a friend's owner-built house in the rainforest. A marsh? In the rainforest? She couldn't believe it. Determined as usual, he'd waved her goodbye one morning, and set off, hitchhiking north.

The clock radio clicked on. She caught the last of the Tasmanian weather forecast: fine and cold, snow on the highlands, sheep alert, bushwalker alert. She dozed a little, then got up.

Under the shower, she thought again about Joe. She'd lost him well before he'd left home, she knew that. One Sunday morning she'd come down to the living room and found him, a ten-year-old, crouched on the big red cushion, still in his pyjamas, watching television. Through the French windows rain soaked black the ivy on the wall, dripped from the ferns onto the pavers. In the television, figures were moving, colours dimming and brightening, tinny television voices dulled by the beat of the rain. He'd looked up at her, then back at the screen as if she didn't exist. Her heart had ached for him, he seemed so lonely, but what could she do?

She got out of the shower. Water steamed from her body in the cold air. She snatched a towel and dried herself as she walked back to her bedroom. George would be here soon.

He arrived after ten, driving a government car.

'You could've let me know you'd be late,' Tessa complained, thinking, cheapskate as usual, won't even use his own car to go to his sick son. She threw her pack onto the back seat and dropped a stack of compact discs into a space beside the gearbox. 'Joe's music.'

'You mean he's got the electric up there?'

'Batteries. Anyway, he's coming back with me.'

'And where might he be coming back to? The stately ruin?' George smirked, pulling away from the kerb and accelerating down the hill.

Tessa looked back at her house, glimpsing the curlicues of its weathered bargeboards through the trees.

'When are you putting the place on the market?'

'Never,' she said. Then, 'How's Sharon?'

'Sharon?'

'Sorry, Shannon, Celia? Your girlfriend.'

'Ancient history.'

She suppressed a smug grin and turned to look out of the windows.

They drove without speaking, cruising through the outer suburbs, through strip development, then to the country, rural towns, more country. Travelling everyday between home and the school where she taught, it was years since Tessa had come out this way.

At Spring Hill on the Midland Highway, roadworks were underway. A truck hosed hot asphalt and a road worker in an orange jacket held up a stop sign. They approached at speed.

'Slow down, George. George!'

The road worker rapidly switched the sign to 'Go'.

Despite herself, Tessa laughed. 'Exercising his power,' she said.

George said, 'Him or me?' Pleased with himself.

Typical egoism, she thought, and couldn't be bothered with an answer.

'Whereabouts is this place Joe's holed up?' he asked.

'Jacky's Marsh. Past Deloraine. It's alternative country.'

'Alternative to what?'

'Just about everything, I suppose.'

'Including us?'

'Looks like it.' She reached for a CD. 'Billy Bragg. Now Valentine's Day is Dead,' she read.

She pushed it into the player and Billy Bragg sang, 'When she first spoke to me my nose began to bleed…'

'Joe's all right really, d'you think?' She leaned towards George.

'Probably out of money,' he said.

'He isn't into money.'

'Everyone's into money. You've got to be, to survive.'

'So that's why you're so tight. Just surviving.'

'That's right, sweetheart.'

They drove off the highway at Ross, parked opposite the Man 'o' Ross Hotel and went inside. A dining room of dark wood and diamond paned windows, odours of steak and gravy. They ordered a counter meal each.

'I'll shout you,' George said.

'I'll pay for myself, thanks.'

'Be independent, then.'

I certainly will, she thought to herself. They ate schnitzel and chips with gravy and downed a beer each, then left. As they drove away, the music started up again. 'I thought about her until the bath water went cold around me...' Tessa laughed, George smiled, and she laughed again, relaxing in the warmth of the car.

The road to Deloraine took them through the backblocks of Cressy with the blue flanks of the Western Tiers on their left mottled with cloud and cloud shadow. A hawk floated above a line of bare poplars. Reaching Cressy, they turned west, rain blurring the countryside. The roads were edged with hawthorn hedges through Bracknell, Cluan, Osmarton, where they once again turned north and she sang along with Billy Bragg: 'One day it happened, she cut her hair and I stopped loving her...'

The farmland gave way to scrubby paddocks and they passed houses, a golf course, more houses and suddenly, Deloraine. Skirting the town, they took the road beside the river.

'Keep a lookout for a weatherboard church,' Tessa said. 'If we reach Meander, we've gone too far.'

They drove beneath Quamby Bluff, marking the northern end of the Tiers, and reached the turn-off to Jacky's Marsh just before the church.

George slowed and pulled the car onto the gravel shoulder. 'How're we going to handle this?' he said, as he yanked the handbrake.

'Handle what?'

'Joe of course.'

'For heaven's sake! It's our son you're talking about.'

'Could be out of it on drugs. You've got to face up to things, Tessa.'

'He's sick, that's all!' She turned her shoulder to him and stared out of the window.

He started the car and they drove along a gravel road through farmland. Ascending, the track deteriorated further. Soon they were tunnelling through dark-leafed undergrowth, water dripping down yellow clay at drain cuttings, the car straddling ruts. George veered off track when a granite boulder protruded from the track. He parked the car and they got out.

'Can't take this vehicle any further.'

'Okay.' Tessa got out, grabbing her backpack. The air was fresh on her cheeks as she started off, walking up the track.

'Know where we're heading?' George caught up with her.

'It's not too far,' she said, trying to sound confident.

The ground was spongy underfoot, making for easy walking, and their breath curled in the cold air. High up wind moved through the trees, the foliage scrolling against clouds touched pink by the sunset. Evening was falling. Tessa hugged herself in her parka, sensing snow. A light shone through the trees.

'Here we are.'

The track continued on, bordered with wattles in bloom to a garden fenced in wire. They veered up a path through the trees to a cottage, and crossed a veranda to the door. As George banged on the door, Tessa looked through the window. A Tilley lamp glowed on a wooden table, fire in a brick fireplace smouldered. Mugs hung on hooks in a dresser, two kitchen chairs were pushed in at the table.

'Looks lovely,' Tessa said. 'So cute.'

George banged on the door again. 'No sign of a welcoming party.'

'He must be close by, he's left the fire.'

'Close by?' George shivered, and looked at the forest rising above the cottage into the night. 'Where might close by be, exactly?'

The cold seeped upwards and Tessa stamped her feet on the boards.

She tried the handle of the door and pushed. It opened, a mat slid across the floor, and inside it smelled of wood smoke and dried herbs. A kettle simmered on the hotplate of a combustion stove.

She hesitated. 'Better take our boots off.'

'You're sure this is okay?' George waited at the open door.

'Of course it's okay.' Tessa eased her feet out of her boots and placed them outside the door.

George wrenched off his boots, they clattered to the boards, and he came in, stooping through the low door. Tessa placed the bag of compact discs on the table, slipped off her coat and backpack, stood with her back to the fire. She couldn't think why Joe wasn't here, but there was nothing they could do but wait for him.

'We could have a cup of tea.' She lifted two mugs off their hooks, found a teapot and took them over to the stove. She opened the tea caddy and made the tea, the steam from the kettle billowing upwards. She refilled the kettle and put it back on the stove. She placed the mugs on the hearth.

George stood awkwardly, his back to the fire, his hands clenched in the pockets of his sheepskin jacket. Tessa pulled a cushion across with her foot, sat on it and gazed into the fire. She took up her mug, warming her hands.

George crouched beside her. 'Surprisingly snug,' he said, 'for an owner-built place, especially with that mezzanine. Whoever built it must've insulated properly.'

They sat in silence for a while, sipping their hot tea. Through the window the foliage was lit a vivid green by the Tilly lamp. Snowflakes twirled down, slowly at first, then faster, settling on the foliage.

'Snowing now,' she said. 'I hope he isn't out in it.' With the warmth of the cottage about her, Tessa felt safe, and at the same time vulnerable, as though only a transparent film lay between her and the freezing night.

'We should've stocked up on snacks before we came up here,' George said.

'There's something in a pot on the stove.'

'Not lentils!'

'Could be broccoli soup.'

'Tempting.'

They laughed, then fell silent.

'Something's happened to him,' Tessa fretted. 'He's up on the Tiers with a broken leg.'

'He rang us, remember. He's okay.' George drew close, comforting her.

'Why did he get us up here, if he's okay?'

'Your guess is as good as mine.'

She stiffened. 'Look up in the mezzanine, George,' she ordered.

'For Christ's sake, Tessa, he would've heard us arrive.' But he climbed the ladder and peered into the space beneath the roof. 'It's a while since he changed the sheets,' he said and jumped down to the floor.

Tessa pulled her sleeping bag out of her pack. George stretched out, leaning on an elbow, and she spread the sleeping bag across him.

'No. You keep it.'

She ignored him, tucking it up, edging closer to him for warmth. 'George, how did this happen?'

'You mean Joe? He's just an independent bastard. Like his mother.'

'Me?'

'That's why you never got on.'

'We always got on.'

'Tessa, I didn't say you didn't love him.'

'And us? What about us, George?'

He faced her. 'I never said I didn't love you.'

She ducked her head and stared into the smouldering fire. 'Why did it happen, then?'

'Dunno.' He looked at her. 'My fault. Should've given you more…' More what?'

Space, time, support… More of everything, I guess.'

She couldn't answer.

The door opened suddenly. Snowy air gusted into the room. A young man stood in the doorway. Snow speckled his head and shoulders, highlighting his clear skin, bright eyes.

'G'day, guys. Made yourselves comfortable? Great!'

'Joe!' Tessa jumped up, the sleeping bag falling around her feet. They hugged. He looked over the top of her head at George.

'Hi, Dad.'

'How are you, son?'

'So you got here okay?'

'Sure,' George said. 'Not much choice…'

'Lovely trip up here,' Tessa said, interrupting him.

A girl appeared from the darkness behind Joe, walking into the light.

Joe turned to her. 'This is Crystal,' he said. 'My olds, Tessa and George.'

They stared at her. She was slight, with sharp eyes that glittered against her white skin and red cheeks. A woollen caftan hung on her shoulders, dusted with snow.

'Hello, Crystal,' Tessa said after a moment.

George grunted, plunging his hands into his pockets.

'I thought you were ill,' Tessa said to Joe, suddenly. 'Is it your asthma?'

'No, Mum…' Exasperated, he turned away from her.

The girl coughed, hacking. She shuddered, and bent over. Joe strode to the tap, ran some water into a glass and handed it to her.

'Would a hot drink help?' Tessa said. 'There's tea in the pot.'

'That's for guests. We don't take caffeinated drinks,' Joe said.

With this answer, Tessa knew there was nothing to be done; it all lay with them. 'I've brought my sleeping bag,' she said and even as she said it, realised this was a mistake.

'Mum…' Joe indicated with his head the lack of room. 'Love to have you. Maybe when I've built another room, hey?'

'You bring us all the way up here?' George turned away.

'There's a good pub down in Deloraine,' Joe said.

'Include me out.' George pulled his coat about him.

Tessa held him back with a hand on his arm, looking from one to the other.

'Call back up tomorrow. We'll have a chat,' Joe said.

George shifted. 'Sorry, mate,' he said. 'Next time. I've got to get back.'

'You do?' Tessa was surprised.

'Work, you know.'

'Right,' Joe said.

There was no offer of food. Tessa picked up her bag, smiled at Crystal, then Joe. George threw the sleeping bag over his shoulder, stooping to pick up the back pack from the floor.

'I'm glad you're well,' Tessa said, and bit her lip. It was clear that right now Crystal was the one not well. 'I brought your CDs up. Love that Billy Bragg.' She looked at him hopefully.

'Billy Bragg? Go, Mum!' and he hugged her. 'Thanks for coming. See you, Dad.'

'Down in Hobart next time, son.'

'Maybe. Want me to guide you to your car?'

'No. You stay inside in the warm, darling.' Tessa kissed him before turning to go.

George bent to pull on his boots and she stumbled into hers, her eyes on Joe. She walked a few steps down the path, looking back. Joe drew Crystal to him. She gave a little wave, he waved back. Tessa remembered again the child watching television that rainy Sunday morning. Her son seemed only able to communicate fleetingly with meanings she grabbed from the night.

'So that's what he wanted us to see,' she understood, now.

'What might that be?'

'He's found someone to care for.'

'Coulda fooled me.'

It wasn't simply that. The burden of illness, deciding what to do with his life, all had been thrown off.

'And he's found this.'

'I'd have taken his word for it,' George said, 'without charging all the way up here to find out.'

'It's the only way he could tell us. It's his way, hey?'

'Maybe.' George was grudging. He draped the sleeping bag around Tessa's shoulders, lifting it up to her cheeks, tucking it around her chin.

Before them the landscape was luminous with snow and the moon hung above in its radiance. Down at the track, a movement of air gusted through wattles drooping with snow, and they exploded one by one, tossing the snow upwards, revealing their dull gold blooms. George's arm was around Tessa's shoulders, and she leaned into him.

'I can see how this could get a hold of you,' George rumbled.

'Yes,' she said. 'It's so beautiful.'

The vast night poured down from the Tiers. They turned and walked down the track, entering a black and white forest of moonlight in snow-hung trees.

'This is exquisite,' Tessa murmured. 'Thank you for bringing us here, Joe.'

'Myrtle stands over there, sassafras, leatherwood…' George intoned.

'You know the names of the trees?'

''Course I do.'

She'd forgotten that about him. 'It's much too late to drive back home, you know.'

'Weather's too bad for driving, anyway.'

'What about your work?'

'Bugger that. I'll take an RDO.'

'Let's go find that pub in Deloraine.'

'You sure?'

'Call back here, on our way home in the morning, George?'

He stopped and gazed into her face.

'To say goodbye to Joe.'

He smiled, she took his hand and together they walked on, into the snowy night.

The Edible Zoo

I'm calling in on Vonnie, my aunt. She sent me a text at lunchtime. 'Bella. Drop in after college. Important.' So I get off the bus and walk through the streets to her place.

Her flat is above an old bakery. Smells of fresh bread waft as I push open the street door, edge past the elephant ears taking over the lobby, dash up the stairs, along the hall, into the kitchen. No smart settings and European appliances here, oh no. Newspapers and books slip and slide across the table – Vonnie reads while she eats. Two wooden dressers are stacked with cracked china plates patterned with kookaburras and koalas crouching in gum leaves. Australiana, worth a heap one day she says. Really? Someone would pay money?

'Vonnie!' Where is she? I skip along the passage to the front room. Nup, she's not there, dive into her bedroom, straight into a rack of retro in chiffon and satin fifties and sixties, her fave decades. Hats! I smack one on, a red pillbox with a feather, wrap a fur stole around my shoulders and there, in the mirror, is me, Ella, not Bella.

Trawl the internet for famous Ellas: there's Ella Fitzgerald, jazz singer, smoky nightclubs, downtown bars, and I hug that stole and croon la lala la… Ella Baker, black civil rights slash human rights activist, author of *Let Nobody Turn Us Around*. Mum would've gone for her, a radical all her life… Ella Cruz, famous model and product endorser, smart, slinky, sassy and in control, she's my choice. Yay!

Mum and her sister Vonnie, what a pair. Wish I had a sister to share everything with, like they did. Both went for life in the cracks and crevices, Vonnie's tiny deck overlooking old warehouses and docks down to a blue glimmer of harbour, a shaft of sky, a square of paved courtyard with a yucca in a pot, perfect! Like the old terrace Dad and

Mum bought cheap when they started out teaching, where our family still lives, its rickety top veranda hogging a million-dollar view across the same beautiful harbour.

My mum and my aunt both loved picking up stuff here and there. That jug is a Campbell, Mum would say, chipped, but look at the glaze; that is a real Persian rug, it's supposed to look tatty; up on the walls art works by famous dudes, unsigned of course. They loved the second-hand, recycled, rescued from tip and skip, both too individual to live ordinary lives, and I'm right there with them. Mum used to say I take after Vonnie, slight, tall, wispy fair hair, eyes set on distant horizons. Kidding. I love her style, but otherwise? I'm more like my Mum , social conscience magnified, weeping at those television ads of starving babies in war-torn countries, saying, if all the governments in the world had a rule that no child will ever be hurt, it'd be the end of war, child abuse and neglect, and men should have their DNA fixed to make it possible and I'm right with her there, my beloved Mum.

'Bella, coffee?' Vonnie's come in from the porch.

'In the bedroom!'

I throw myself onto her bed – get this, a water bed! So seventies! Bounce up and down and then, right there on the bedside table – Nude 12 ultra-thin condoms for the natural feeling. My aunt? Has sex? Safe sex? Kidding! I yank the packet and out one springs, thin, slippery, limp, so clownish yet so serious, reminding me of bubblegum, birthday balloons, bums, and all the other 'b's in the world. But what's it doing here? My aunt has a secret life? She's a tour leader for wealthy retiree vacationers, just got back from a trip to China and Mongolia. In fact, the photos – yes, photos, she's that retro – are on the coverlet with brochures for another season of touring: *Undiscovered Italy for Discerning Travellers*: shots of cheerful oldies creaking on zimmer frames down a cobbled street. Or glamorous oldies looking so clean and healthy on the deck of a luxury cruise ship. No sign of disease, breakdown, cancer with any of them.

Vonnie comes in with the coffees. She dumps a mug on the side table and shiny magazines slide to the floor. I grab it as she plumps down beside me in her kindly but glum way, blonde-grey hair bundled, crocs clunking to the floor. Yes, she wears crocs! While she's hugging a beautiful silk oriental-style housecoat, she's so for real!

'How's it going, Vonnie?'

'Two weeks to go, before my next trip.'

'Where to?'

'European cities, Baltic, Prague, Tallin, Riga, then Helsinki, ending up in St Petersburg.'

'Sounds wonderful!'

'Like herding cats, these oldies, they know their own minds.'

'Wish I was going with you.'

'I know, darling.' She takes my hand.

Oh my god, I know what's coming, a lecture. Drugs, internet porn, binge drinking, sex, the evils of smoking, my career goal, take your pick. She thinks I'm flighty, about to go off the deep end, so not me.

'And how are you coping?'

'School's fine,' I say, batting her words away.

'Studying hard?'

'Sure.' And that's the truth. I want to get free of that place, it's stifling.

'How's your social life?'

'Oh, you know…' My best mate is Sophie, she's cool. We were planning on backpacking around Australia this Christmas break, fruit picking before we got real jobs or started uni, but then I backed out. There's my dad, you see, and Ben.

'All good then.' She gazes at me, and I can tell she doesn't believe a word.

'Got to go. Homework, nice catching up.' I jerk free, the bed lurches, we roll sideways and clutch each other.

How does she get a good night's sleep? Turn over suddenly in the middle of the night and this thing would just take off! Floating out the window and down the street, to the harbour, bobbing all the way to Antarctica.

'Bella!

'Vonnie!' I burst into giggles as we topple upright.

The wave has carried my hat across the room, my stole dangles across the mirror. I know, I exaggerate, but why not?

'Finish your coffee, be a sweetheart.'

Gulping it down hot, I try again. 'Really, got to head off, no one's home, Ben and Dad…'

'You're doing such a good job, but listen, darling…'

'Yeah?' Is she going to offer to take me on this trip?

'We need to chat.'

'Oh.' I try not to say what about, but it's like holding your breath. 'What about?' I burst out.

'Choices. Your choices.'

I sigh. What can the old scallop tell me? I love Vonnie. She's chaotic, eccentric, loving, but what can she know about my life?

'What's this about?' I wave the condom packet to sideline the serious.

'Ah yes. Condoms, dear.'

'So?'

'You've got to protect yourself. Young blokes don't have the nous. You can't put your trust in a spotty toe rag.'

'Vonnie!' I screech at her and she squints, hurt. Oh god, Mum'd tear strips off me. 'I know about this stuff.'

'Are you…?'

'Am I…? And derail her again. 'What are these?' Thrust a photo at her.

'Oh!' And she's away. 'The White Swan Hotel in Guangzhou.' She holds it up. 'One of the great hotels of the world.'

It looks it, this massive place with colonnades towering amongst trees. I pick another, a photo of an alleyway stacked with wicker baskets, bins, basins, and towers of bird cages at the back.

'Chinese medicine,' Vonnie says. 'In the Qing Ping Market, just down from the hotel.'

'Cool.'

'It's called the Edible Zoo.'

'The edible what?'

'These baskets and basins, darl. They're heaped with what looks like bundles of twigs but no, they're bunches of fried centipedes, or millipedes. Next are dried beetles. Cockroaches. Grasshoppers, monkey skeletons.'

'Shiish!' I gulp my coffee as Vonnie picks out another photo.

'The live animal section.'

'Uh oh! No thanks!' But she's unstoppable.

'Fish, snakes, cats kept alive in cages, tied up or in sacks, the Chinese like their meat fresh, they don't have refrigeration. The market is the abattoir in effect.'

'Got to get home. Like, right now.'

'You're walking along,' she's on a roll, 'someone buys a cat or a pangolin or a raccoon.'

'Wild animals too?'

'Nothing's spared. They whip the animal out, bash it on the concrete, dunk it into boiling water, skin it and hand it over so fast you can only gasp.'

I gasp.

'You need a strong stomach. Blood everywhere.'

I do not have a strong stomach. 'Thanks for the coffee.' I leap to make my escape, the bed surges and the photos cascade to the floor.

'I've made an appointment for you, with my doc.' She leans to grab me. 'Fill you in on contraception, safe sex, STDs, personal health…'

'We covered it at school first year,' and I make a dash for it.

'Worse than useless, school sex education.' She scoots down the hall after me like a mad woman, the appointment card clutched in her claw as I dive down the stairs. 'Help you to check for lumps, you know… Your mother, your grandmother…'

Oh god. When am I going to get free of all that! I just want to be left alone, but I snatch the card, just to get away. 'See you, Vonnie,' and I'm out of there, the door crashing behind me.

Walking home, I go over and over my mum's illness – breast cancer. I didn't understand; she had to suffer so she could get well? Getting the best treatment the specialists had meant radiation burns? Her hair falling out? The headscarf she wore like a flag, so proud, so brave. She didn't want remission, she wanted a cure, but remission is what she got, and for a year we were back to normal and I was flying, I knew all I had to do was believe, and she'd come through. Her hair grew back curly; check my chemo curls she laughed. We were so happy, she was getting better. What is happiness? I used to think it was things, new tight jeans, new iPhone... No. It was Mum, back from illness. But for Mum, staring at me as if she never wanted to lose sight of me, hugging Ben as if she never wanted to let go of him, that was happiness. Us, her kids. Her life. Our family's future.

Then the cancer was back. Metastasised: how I hate that word! It means it spread, from her breasts to her bones, everywhere, like poison. She didn't want to eat, spent hours out walking Faithful Dog Pedro, our little dog, but even that stopped. Dad, poor Dad! He moved out to the spare room with the junk, leaving her their bedroom, its French doors and deck a cool quiet refuge. Loving her to bits, doing everything he could, reducing his days teaching. She joined the pink brigade, finding solace with other sufferers, walking, rowing, but I wasn't fooled by it. I'm telling you, I'll never wear pink again!

For Vonnie too, her best friend, her sister, it meant going with her to endless hospital visits, clinging to time spent together as it dwindled away. Last few weeks for Mum, she moved in, nursing her. Dad had finally finished the en suite in the bedroom he'd started years ago, and Mum was so grateful, poor Mum losing so much weight, so weak.

My mother used to write me notes, put them under my pillow, before she got too ill: 'Shine bright my komodo princess'. I still find them on scraps of paper caught in clumps of dust under my bed. She'd always wanted to be a writer, and a singer, she used to sing all day, Joanie's 'I wish I had a river', and Nina. Not Nina Simoaning, Dad used to say to nark her. You try living as a black woman in America, Mum'd retort.

To me, the to and froing of my parents, songs, chat, Ben's computer games pinging and racketing in the background, Faithful Dog Pedro barking, were the sounds of daily life that became tainted with the ever-present cancer. Like, Mum loved scrambled eggs and bacon, so now, nuh, can't eat them, the smell… She took up yoga, meditation at dawn, so I got up early too, instead of lying in, was never home late from school, in case. I'd sneak in, quietly, catch her by surprise, writing her diary. She'd hide it, but I read it. Once and only once.

Today I'm cut up, poisoned, fried, sore, tired, hot, grumpy, no bull shit scrubbing helps me minimise my lymphoedema build-up. Scrubbing! Floors, bench tops, shower screen…so much that's scrubbable in life but I can't scrub away illness…

Then:

LVI is present means that they see tumour cells within blood or lymphatic cells in the sample they are testing. This does not necessarily mean that the tumour cells are travelling my body. It just increases the chances that they may be. Fuck!

I've still got her journal. It's in my drawer waiting for some time when I have the courage to read it cover to cover and walk her journey. Promise, Mum, I whisper. I'll be your Ella Baker, activist, fighting for peace and justice, a writer too.

Jason and Mel the palliative care team in the last weeks were such a help, giving her poor wasted body sponge baths, showing Vonnie how to administer the painkiller through this tube thing in her arm, lowering the bed so she didn't fall out.

Vonnie had cried buckets during the memorial, everyone, me too: that video montage! Shots of the cutest, sportiest, wildest, out-there girls dancing, splashing in the surf, demonstrating with placards: Stop the Franklin, women against war, homes for refugees. The magic of seeing your mother in the ancient history before you were born, this passionate, determined woman, I was so proud of her. Then with me and Ben as babies, toddlers, school mugshots, growing and changing,

Mum mellowing, taking to cooking, gardening, sitting out there reading with Dad. Did she regret anything? No, she'd never regret anything in her life. Not my wife, Dad said, as the video ended and the last song started, the Beatles, and everyone's bawling as they sing 'There are places I'll remember… With lovers and friends I still recall, some are dead and some are living, in my life I've loved them all…'

The house is silent as I come in through the front door. Ben is home, his school bag is lying in the hall. He's probably out with Faithful Dog Pedro, such a good kid, handling it. Dad, I just can't get through to him, locked away in his grief. I go upstairs, throwing my bag down, and stretch out on the veranda, taking in the sounds of the town rising with the late afternoon heat.

My period's due, the ache's starting, the pain, the swelling, the hormones, the tampons, blood everywhere, I can't stand it! It's about illness, this female body, cancer, being eaten from within, STDs. My only protection? Condoms, slick membranes between ease and disease, flaccid as the gall bladders of skinned snakes, IUDs with insect-like feelers travelling the secret pathways of my body, pills controlling my hormones, packets crackling like insect carapaces? Too much! Can't I get myself neutralised, sterilised, hysterectomised? Ella Cruz, famous model and product-endorser wouldn't stand for it, so I recite the names of all the skincare products promising eternal beauty and health I can think of: Lancome, Clinique, Dove, Guerlain, Estee Lauder… Because I don't want to grow older, change, become someone else. I want to stay the same for Mum, her girl. But then, go for it, Mum always said. Don't compromise. For me, Bella, for me.

The air cools, everyday sounds rise up: a motorbike revving down at the corner, a dog barking next door, kids shouting, cars passing, the real world. The front door slams, someone's home and I sit up, get myself together, time to get us a meal on the table.

'Promise, Mum, I'll go for it. Right now. I'll do us a beautiful bolognese,' I whisper, 'fresh salad, parmesan and pasta.' And I get up to go inside, and run down to the kitchen. Cheerful, capable, on task. Her Bella.

Cull Island

The day was hot. At the jetty, a ferry ran its engines before taking tourists out on the morning's Marineland Wildlife Tour. The end of the jetty formed a T where a forty-foot ketch was moored. Lines slung from the boat to projecting rocks on the jetty road kept it from drifting. These ropes, splashing in and out of the water, threw herringbone patterns of rust and blue on the white sand of the ocean floor that Anna, when she wasn't deep in her book, found mesmerising.

From the shade of the companionway of the ketch, Anna watched Bert, the ferryman, hurry along the jetty, a green bucket swinging from his hand. Lowering her book, she watched as a tourist coach drew up with a blast of its horn. A minute later, one by one, tourists stepped down from the bus into the blinding sunshine. Their lowered eyes gave them an air of reverence as if blessed with the benediction of sunlight. Chatting and smiling, they strolled along the jetty in two and threes. Anna rubbed a hand across her hot forehead as the tourists passed by, then on a whim stood, slipped on sandals and stepped to the bow of the boat. She grabbed the mooring rope, braced her legs and pulled the boat against the surge to the jetty. The bowsprit plunged. She teetered on it as it rose up, then jumped across to the jetty's boards. The tourists thronged around her as she walked down the gangplank onto the ferry and dropped some money into the green bucket.

On board, Anna leaned against the rail, facing the tourists where they sat on green-painted benches. Bert shouted to Max, his offsider, who flung the mooring rope back onto the jetty, and the ferry turned and chugged out into the bay. A light wind rising off the water feathered Anna's face, giving her slight relief from the headaches that dogged her. The public address system crackled.

Bert coughed into the microphone for attention. He introduced himself and welcomed them to the cruise. 'Boy, oh boy,' he enthused, 'we're going to have a great time on our Marineland Wildlife Tour. It's a fantastic region, an archipelago of islands, a national park, on the very edge of the Great Southern Ocean. Home to orca and humpbacks, manta rays and deep sea turtles, who knows what we might see!'

Anna gazed up at the wheelhouse as Bert pointed out landmarks on the shore: a gaping hole in the tanker wharf where a bulk oil carrier had failed to stop; a boat, the smallest ever to compete in the annual Sydney to Hobart Yacht Race, a blue water classic; the Rotary Memorial Lookout on a scrubby headland. Running out of distinctive features, Bert's voice stuttered, the PA clicked off, and the ferry idled up the headland towards the islands standing flat on the horizon.

Tourists had snapped pictures as Bert listed his trivia. Peering over the edge of her book, Anna studied them. Most were older, raked thin and leathery, or smooth, oily and corpulent. They were dressed in brand-new outfits, self-consciously coordinated. The few younger ones looked out of place, and there were no children. But then, it wasn't the school summer holidays. On the centre bench sat a row of white-haired couples dressed in fawn and pale blue, who turned in unison like geriatric carnival clowns to view the sights. A couple in bubblegum-pink matching leisure suits moved about the boat together, as if glued. A man, flesh oozing from orange stubbies and a navy singlet, panted on the wheelhouse steps, while a dark woman rigid as angle iron in a black halter-neck and tights stubbed out a cigarette on the rail by him.

American voices reached Anna from the stern, the men growling, the women shrill. Two tall women, thin armed, gaunt necks projecting, walked past in a glitter of rings, necklaces and bracelets. They raised white-framed sunglasses to look about as if surveying the savanna for prey. Anna shrank behind her book.

Turning back to the rail, Anna watched the headland slip by. It fell away to a point, a jumble of massive boulders above shelves of rock licked black by the ocean. Mustard algae edged foam laced shallows of aquamarine deepening to blue.

The PA clicked on and Bert called for the tourists' attention. 'Only last week,' he said, his voice breathy with awe, 'a young Swedish tourist, beautiful girl, slipped off the black rock into the water. Snatched to her death by the ocean, a tragedy. Nobody could save her.'

Gasps, a thrill, went through the tourists. They rushed to the ferry's side, snapping pictures with their phones. Of what? Anna wondered. She imagined the girl plunging through the net of light, as frail, blonde and insubstantial as the reflection into which she merged. But why couldn't they save her? Where was the dinghy? Anna looked back to check. No dinghy bobbed along behind the ferry.

'Beware, everybody!' Bert exhorted. The dangerous black rock. Looks safe, but boy oh boy, it is deadly.'

Suddenly Anna longed for the solitude of evening on the ketch, soothed by the click of barnacles opening and closing on the steel hull, the constant surge of water against the bow, the tap of rigging against the aluminium mast. In the darkness, her pain swollen in the daytime world receded, the pain of her break-up, the madness that had engulfed her one night last summer.

Sam had taken her to a restaurant down in Fremantle for dinner to celebrate her birthday. Driving back to Perth, the night was so beautiful they'd parked the car and walked across the Horseshoe Bridge to a wine bar in Beaufort Street. The air was balmy, and people just out from the movies and the theatre crowded the streets. The wine bar was packed and Anna wanted to go somewhere less crowded, but they'd been seen by Siobhan, a workmate of Sam's, who was drinking with a university lecturer who Anna disliked. Anna had smiled briefly as they'd pushed their way in, and then moved along the bar. Sam bought her a gin and tonic, himself a glass of red. At what point had she lost him? Thinking back, she remembered he was still with her as she sipped her drink, but when she turned around he was gone. She'd heard jazz piano, looked through the crowd, thinking he might be there.

Then Siobhan had come over and stood by her. 'You know Dermott?' she asked Anna.

'Yes…' Glanced along the bar to Dermott, the lecturer. He raised his glass, ironically Anna thought at the time.

'He's a great asset to the university,' Siobhan said.

Anna didn't answer. Where on earth was Sam?

'Don't you agree?'

Anna ignored her, and gazed through the red glare of lights, trying to locate Sam.

'Is that a yes?'

'No,' she said. 'It's a no.'

'Who are you to think that?' Siobhan clutched at her glass, her red hair wild. She was drunk, Anna realised.

'I'll think what I like, I do most of the time.' Anna gulped the rest of her drink and made to move away.

'These might help your thinking processes.'

Anna glanced back at her, and watched as her hand delved into her bag. Red-tipped fingers emerged slowly, tantalisingly from the bag, holding an envelope. Out came a swatch of colour photos. The woman flipped them fanwise, as if inviting Anna to choose one, any one… It was night, and in one after another Sam was featured in his work suit, open-collared, tie awry, slumped at a wrought-iron table littered with glasses and wine bottles. More people were sitting at tables behind him, and drinking beside a swimming pool. He was with Siobhan. Aqua reflections thrown up from the pool dappled her bare shoulders. In one photo she leaned towards him, her chin tilted. He was drunk, but below the drunkenness he had the look, Anna thought, of a captive. In the last photo, Siobhan leaned triumphantly between Sam and Dermott, her dress scooped low, her breasts, the arch of her throat…

The noise of the wine bar roared in Anna's ears, bitter fluid seeped into her mouth and she bent from intense pain in the pit of her stomach. She lunged for the photos, but the red-nailed hand slid the photos into the envelope, back into her bag.

'None of this would've happened…'

She didn't want to hear the poison flowing from this woman's mouth.

'He's out the back, chatting up one of Dermott's students,' Siobhan spat. 'When you find your Sam, tell him from me he can keep his bloody ring!' She ripped a ring off her finger. It glittered as she threw it to the floor.

Anna got to the door and burst out into the street, started off in the wrong direction, turned back towards the pulsating lights and laughter, into the path of a taxi. It braked, she staggered against it, got in and headed home.

Sam, this stranger she lived with, came in at about dawn. He wouldn't answer her accusations, her demands, then admitted it all before staggering out, leaving her for good.

Evenings, she sat on the deck of the ketch. Land, ocean, sky merged into planes of blue. Anna's brother Steve, who owned the ketch, sat with her sharing drinks, wrapping her in a rug, soothing her, then losing patience, telling her Sam was a sod, she was better off without him, to get over it. She tried to explain, it wasn't being on her own, she wasn't lonely. It was the malice, the careless destruction of her life, of her trust, her love. What had brought that down on her?

She stayed up late. The wind flowed endlessly out of star-pointed night, black waters poured ceaselessly below. In this blackness her connection to the shore was as tenuous as the mooring ropes that held the bucking ketch. She kept her eyes on the horizon, where two green navigation lights flashed through the night, out of sync, in unison and then out of sync, the cycle continuing endlessly until dawn seeped up from the horizon and she rolled into a bunk until the sun was hot.

'Keep a sharp lookout for porpoises!' Bert admonished over the PA.

Max stood in the bow, his arm held out like a plank, indicating islands as Bert named them.

'Rabbit Island, Rat Island, Cat Island. You won't find a rabbit on

Rabbit Island,' he said. 'The rats got the rabbits and the cats got the rats. The national park rangers shot up the cats and everything else not listed as native. Boy oh boy, they'll be shootin' us up next!'

The islands slid by. Hot, hostile, their flanks were streaked tan and olive. On the deck, a man dug a stone out of his wife's sandal. From the wheelhouse came a bellow as the fat man flopped in the shade. The dark woman sat at an angle and lit another cigarette. The couple in pink appeared to have melted into each other, but in the stern the American voices were as persistent as cicadas. Picnic baskets were corralled on the benches, with cheese, fruit, cake, bread and dips.

A voice complained, 'You've forgotten the flask, Mum. You've gone and forgotten the iced tea!'

A cluster headache shot arrows of pain above her eyes. Anna lifted her book for shade from the glare. She looked across the deck. The happy couples were a gallery of the weird and banal, yet they were the chosen ones, still married, she guessed, blessed with the rectitude of the ordinary. Had it been from a vision of this that Sam had fled?

'Cull Island,' Bert announced.

The ferry entered a north-facing bay where the heat, trapped by the curve of the shore, rebounded off a barrier of green.

'In the thirties, we used to bring the sheep out here. Fun and games getting them onto the island,' Bert laughed. 'See that iron bar over there?'

Fifteen metres away, where the water met the black rocks, a right-angled rusty bar protruded, dripping above the wash of foam.

'Bit of slipway there.'

Tourists angled their phones for the best shots.

'Got the sheep up the slipway onto the island. Fattened them up. Culled 'em.' Bert looked over the tourists, waiting, and the query came from an American.

'Culled, sir? What do you mean?'

'Slaughtered them one by one for the township. Kept the whole place going during the Depression. Something always turns up when times are hard, I find.'

'Thank you,' came the polite reply.

'We'll nudge in close to get a good look.'

Obediently, the tourists gathered at the rail.

'Goats, introduced of course, Cape Barren geese, oystercatchers,' Bert intoned, though nothing living was visible. 'Around the point an old sea lion's got his favourite rock. He likes to sun himself, and oh boy, does he tiddly wink – the smell is terrific. See that grey bush? Box furze, introduced from South Africa. The bright green, that's stinkweed spread here from the mainland. Used to be big seabird colonies, burnt out by the fishermen. Anyone seen a goat?'

Someone shouted, the tourists bunched together, phones and cameras ready.

'Right,' Bert ordered, 'I want you to use your imaginations. Max, ready?'

Max got to the rail and held out an arm as Bert reeled off directions.

'See that white patch high up? Look to the left, a big boulder, follow the line of stinkweed down some rocks, shade, a cave. Could be some Cape Barren geese there, sheltering from the heat!'

More excited shouts, but Anna couldn't locate the white patch in the glare. To her, the island appeared entirely lifeless, its turquoise shallows seeping into the black ocean like blood, reminding her of places she'd read about in the Pacific. Blasted points of land where the spirits of the dead walked on their journey from this life to the next. Why had she come on this absurd tour when she could be cooling off on the boat? It had seemed a reasonable thing to do, but hadn't the whole of her life been one of reason, leading her to…what? This time and place among strangers, mourning the end of her life with Sam.

Listlessly, Anna shifted along the rail. Leaning out to catch the lift of cool air off the water, she glimpsed a smear of white in the growth above the shoreline. Through the shimmer of light was the shape of a bird against the olive-green undergrowth. Its head still, beak curved, scimitar wing folded, the only fixed point in the radiation of heat, the dance of light, a raptor as solitary as a totem. Anna waited for Bert to announce the sighting of the first living creature for the whole tour, looked up the wheelhouse, only to see his blank face turned towards her.

Anna looked back at the bird and understood. The sounds of the ferry, the clamour of the tourists receded, replaced by a certainty that this was a stage in her journey, a shedding of the old, of all previous meaning in her life, a chance to swim free into solitude, days and nights blurring in timeless rhythms, leaving behind on the shore the routines and habits of her life for the simple actions of living, thinking, feeling.

The splash was slight. But Bert heard Anna go, and twisted round to look. Surfacing, her head was sleek, she was swimming strongly. She'd make it up the landing stage onto Cull Island just fine. He'd picked her out, first time she surfaced on the yacht moored by the jetty. Gone by every day, jingling the money in his green bucket, making sure she noticed. Sure enough, she'd swallowed the bait and taken the trip. Now she'd gone overboard. No need to rush into a rescue. Tomorrow, when the bloke on the yacht raised the alarm, he could stage a massive hunt through the islands. A real event. Terrific word of mouth, fantastic for ticket sales, for the community as a whole.

'Time to feed the fish!' he announced quickly, easing the ferry around and heading out of the bay. 'Watch now while Max feeds the marine life. Sunfish, stingray, turtle, they're all here on the Marineland Wildlife Tour of the islands, where you'll have the time of your life.' He smiled, replaced the mike and, without a backward look, turned off the PA.

Bethlehem in Sydney

It's my first day in Sydney. I'm up for Christmas from Hobart, staying with a friend, Philip, in Elizabeth Bay. Philip has a Moreton Bay fig growing in his flat. Massed leaves press the corners, elephant limb branches heave through the rooms, aerial roots splay across the walls, reducing windows to chinks of light in the jungle, Philip's art to cave paintings, the television to a visual stutter.

Forget all that. The Moreton Bay fig is bonsai. Perfect in detail, it inhabits an enamel dish on a window ledge ten storeys up. There's no jungle here; it's a shift in attention that allows the jungle in.

After breakfast, I met a friend in the Botanical Gardens. He's much older than I am, so we played the girls' own game of schoolgirl from the upper fifth and uncle (secretly her lover) out for a treat. He bought me a pavlova in the restaurant, I ate it sitting on the lawn, where he pulled my hair into pigtails. A group of Chinese tourists circled past, browsing on the scenery, necks craned for camera angles. They looked at us as if we were some exotic breed. You know why we're doing this, I said. It's because we're writers. The jungle is our habitat. He said he didn't know what I was talking about, slipped his hand along my thigh to test the elastic in my navy school knickers, found I had none on, leaned across and sucked at my pavlova. Cameras clicked.

Heading back to Elizabeth Bay, I found I'd lost my purse in the Botanical Gardens. Catch a taxi and pay when you get here, Philip said when I rang him. Christmas Eve, it was difficult to get a taxi, but I did; the driver was a Palestinian from Gaza.

Exactly ten years ago, I was in Bethlehem for Christmas Eve. I'd driven there with some Australian friends from the kibbutz. To get into the

Square of the Holy Manger where the birth of Christ was being celebrated, we had to check through a security booth, were frisked and our bags were checked by armed soldiers. Up on the rooftops, black against the sunset, commandoes prowled.

In the square, hundreds of volunteers from kibbutzim milled, lit by arc lights. We looked for the Christmas tree and the choir. No Christmas tree, no choir, no carols. The music filling the square was recorded born-again harmonies. Some Canadian volunteers told me that a mass was taking place in the Church of the Nativity. We pushed through the crowd but the doors were closed shut. In the middle of the square, an American televangelist stood in a pool of white light. His camel hair coat hung open; underneath was a cashmere jumper, and with his silver hair and tan, he looked opulent. He turned from side to side, with a dazzling smile for the network television crews, lighting the crowd with his charisma.

I pushed my way to the little lit stalls edging the square, where Arabs were selling cheap holy figurines made of olive wood. I chose a Christ on a donkey, haggled with the stallholder. He was a Palestinian from Gaza with a family, he told me. I gave him the price. Nearby, a guide brought a group of American tourists to trestle tables where food could be bought. The tourists were plump and middle-aged, and perched uncomfortably on tubular-steel stools. The guide talked non-stop and we smirked as he handed out chicken and falafel and said it was kosher, taking double the usual price from the gullible Christians. The brotherhood of man, I asked? The stallholder laughed and pushed back half my money.

The taxi reached Philip's block of flats in Elizabeth Bay Road, and I asked the taxi driver, could he wait while I went up to get some money. I had no money on me. No! He had a fare out to Bankstown, $55. Just wait, the crook said, I get the money. He run away! No fare! The police do nothing! But I've lost my purse, I said. You leave something here, of value, for me. Something worth money? My shoes. Worth fifty dollars.

I hooked them off, handed them over and padded away. Philip and I came back with the fare, and a couple of cold bottles of beer which we drank with the taxi driver for Christmas. I told him about the Palestinian from Gaza I'd met one Christmas in Bethlehem. Probably my brother, he said.

So now I'm leaning out of Philip's window drying my hair in the tenth-floor stream of warm polluted air, with evening deepening over the harbour. Something is going on at the yacht club down at Rushcutter's Bay. Roman torches and barbecue flares flame up, figures move across bright windows in the clubhouse, the steady thump thump of music reaches me. I'm going over later, I yell at Philip. Hook myself a cruising merchant banker.

At eleven, the barbecue's finished, families have taken kids home, hard-drinking yachties, men and women, are getting their fill before a big race tomorrow. I saunter along the marina to check the international maxis. A shout from the clubhouse brings me back. A cabaret has started, crewmen from different yachts are putting on acts. Everybody's crowded into the upstairs room, the air is fetid with heat and sweat. 'You give me head' pounds out. I push through and get up on a chair. A guy is prancing about. A life-sized doll is swinging from his hand. Blue eyes with stitched lashes are wide, acrylic blonde pigtails swing; beneath her gingham dress her pink tube legs and club feet dangle helplessly. He tosses her about, kisses her red felt lips, the men yell for more and sway forwards. He grabs the doll's chest, the music pounds, he strokes her legs. The crewmen shout advice. The dancer rolls his eyes, pushing his hand up the doll's dress, then straddles her onto his fly. The men roar as she falls backwards, pigtails jerking as he dances around. I've had enough, fall off the chair and struggle to the door, burst out into the night. It's after midnight, Christmas Day now.

Walking back to the flat around Rushcutter's Bay, I feel outrage, but also a creeping complicity. I'm too willing to go halfway in this violence, and I feel ashamed. For them, for me. The night rings with the chink and chime of rigging against the masts of the yachts moored there, and it's like walking past a glass forest alive with bellbirds. Tomorrow, the racing yachts will stream across the harbour, dazzling against sky and water, spinnakers blooming as they go about, while upstairs in an empty room, a doll lies in a mess of vomit, ash and spilled booze, legs twisted together, arms and pigtails flung out, blue eyes staring upwards. See, a shift in attention allows a crucifixion, now or two thousand years ago.

The Advertisement

Three days ago, Lisa answered an advertisement. Eschewing online sites, she'd hunted it down in the personal column of the local newspaper. She rang and made an appointment. Now, she sings in the shower, smoothes soapy hands across her breasts and considers the possibilities. The advertisement:

> Older Man, Experienced, Educated. Has everything, seeks a companion of Sense and Sensibility for Meetings Pleasant and Rewarding [his caps].

As a college English teacher, Lisa had noted the distinctive placement of the adjectives, and the title of one of Jane Austen's novels. *Sense and Sensibility.* Sounds reassuringly free, she thinks, of the cues for romance. Lisa is too old, too cynical, too independent for romance, she tells me as I hold out the warmed bath towel for her. Observe how impatiently she turns off the taps and steps out of the shower stall. Are her thoughts slithering out of control towards candlelight and soft music? If not, she may have missed other hidden messages lying beneath the studied innocence of the words. The only code built into this type of advertisement, surely, is that inherent in form, and form determines content, as she teaches every day in her English classes. The style of the advertisement leaves room only for clichés, she states, but the style is what else but romantic?

In the bedroom, spread out on the doona, are Lisa's leather slacks and her silk shirt. Outside, the air is cold. It could snow later and she will need the thick pink socks which she is pulling on. She snaps on her underclothes, bra and pants, tosses the silk shirt in the air and slips it on as it flutters down. She pulls on her leather slacks and fastens them firmly. At the mirror, I brush her hair dry, and then I plait it loosely and wind it up on her head. She stains her lids with violet eyeshadow, mascaras her lashes, dabs on pink lipstick which matches her socks, takes a look at herself then swings out into the hall. There, she pulls on her boots, wraps a mohair scarf around her shoulders, takes a hooded coat off a hook and opens the front door, where she pauses to shrug on her coat.

While she is standing in the doorway, consider: her preparations have been careful for the assignation and she looks good, but she certainly hasn't overdone the allure. Wouldn't high heels, a voluptuous look and an arrival in a taxi be more winning for an older man who has everything? Or are her sturdy boots and her warm coat a protective camouflage with which she must be enticed, with patient but persistent pressure into surrendering? She checks for keys and money and with a wave leaves, closing the door behind her.

Watch her walking through the streets, on her way to the cathedral in the city, where James will pick her up in his Saab. She strides through the crackling air, her breath gusting . What do you think, does she look too obviously 'a Professional Woman mid-thirties. Enjoys music, literature, leisurely walks'? Quite possibly, but crossing the kerb into the darkness of the buildings at once she is 'Anonymous. Unknown. A Person of Unrevealed Possibilities.'

Crossing the broad lit areas of Salamanca Place, under bare plane trees lit by fairy lights, she heads towards the floodlit tower of the cathedral, whose bells peal into the night. She stops with the lights at an intersection at the top of the street, you know the one, where in colonial times the stone buildings on the near corner were the courts, and the prison was on the opposite corner: prison, courts and cathedral face each other, and in the middle of the road where now there is a traffic island, stood the gibbet, the intersecting point of life, death and eternity.

Lisa waits for the green light, the walk sign, signalling the shuffle back to the prison for the reprieved. And the red stop sign? At the gibbet, of course. See how reality operates here? Planes shift, and lost times, submerged meanings reveal themselves. The secular controls the sacred and the profane, closer in style to gulag realism than European romance or ecclesiastical righteousness.

A Saab, silver under the street lights, glides around the corner behind Lisa as she crosses the road. She doesn't notice it until it U-turns and cruises back to the opposite corner. It parks, red parking lights, a cigarette glows in the dark interior, lighting a hand, the hint of a profile. He smokes? The driver's door opens and a man gets out. He is tall, conservatively dressed, mature. Bland almost, with no hint of threat about him, rather a touch of ennui. Lisa steps back, seeking shadows, for her fear is of respectability, its negation of contact, its obsession with surfaces, the soft violence that lies beneath it. But, what the hell. She crosses the road, they chat, and she gets into the car. This is against the rules for a first meeting. But you can guess the reason: it's too cold to hang around and, on a Monday night, there's nowhere much to go. This leads to the second transgression: after exchanging names – James, Lisa – she agrees to go to his place for a coffee. Only a short distance out of the city, he says.

The Saab slides away from the kerb. On the way out of town, they cut through Lisa's suburb. Yes, she nods, this is where she lives. She asks him his profession. Optometrist, he replies, and Lisa is impressed. She imagines firm dry hands, impeccably suited to fit constructs of wire and glass, arcing across opaline skin, slender arm pieces inserted behind the Gothic roll of the ear, where the hair catches painfully. And herself? An English teacher. Oh? No questions about that, and she prickles, suddenly wanting out of there. But they are heading further away from the city, driving around bushy hillsides. They lurch right into a private drive, travel a short distance through trees and turn right again, skidding on gravel, to a stop. The countryside falls away to shadowed hills where the moon is rising. To Lisa, it is a spot demanding a turreted Victorian country mansion whose thylacine occupants are the survivors of family horror, a house of the type still to be found decaying at places no longer marked on the map, places with names like Lower Marshes. Instead, the headlights reveal bare ground, concrete steps, a panelled front door lit by a cone of yellow light, the entrance to a triple-fronted brick and tile villa. It is so very Australian, and her heart sinks.

Lisa glances at James and unfastens her seat belt. He turns obliquely towards her. His silhouette is calm, dignified, even.

'I like to get the details out of the way beforehand,' she hears him say. 'As an English teacher, you must have understood the meaning of my advertisement. I think two hundred dollars will suffice.'

A price? For what? It is now that the subliminal becomes conscious and the code in the advertisement is cracked. Remember the words 'pleasant and rewarding'? Lisa has pressed the hidden button and reality opens before her, like a false bookcase hiding a pederast's den. She looks from James to the house in disbelief. A movement catches her eye. The neatly panelled front door is opening, and as she watches, a darkness lit eerily behind shows the distorted silhouette of a human figure.

At this point, let us consider the style of this story. Has romance indeed become Gothic, revealing a tale of horror and perversion? Is Lisa about to become the terrified heroine who flees the doomed castle but never quite escapes? One of de Sade's innocent victims, a Justine rather than a Juliette? But who is the predator and whom the victim? The roles, as you and I know, are interdependent, interchangeable even. But now, Lisa reacts with flight and she has the car door open. She tears away from James's grasp, his cry of 'Wait!' Falls out onto the gravel and is off, down the drive. Behind her, lights slash on and off, and a car door slams. She veers up a bank and fights through the undergrowth edging the track, and into open forest. Like a deer, Lisa instinctively knows when to freeze. She stops, allowing her breathing to slow. Voices recede into the night, lost in the vast darkness flooding down. A car engine starts up. She follows the sound, watches as headlights flicker as it departs down the drive, and estimates her distance from the road.

Above, the forest canopy scrolls against low cloud moving in from the west. The moon lights the mottled trunks of gums, granite outcrops blotched with lichen, the forest floor. She passes through a landscape which in its grainy black and white reality is the landscape of dream and fantasy, familiar from her childhood, and the illustrations of Grimm and Andersen. The landscape of flight, but also of refuge and she is at ease with its muted tones, its damp scents of mould and eucalyptus, its vast silence and tiny sounds.

A short while later, Lisa jumps down onto the highway. The air is warmer now and she loosens her scarf. She sets off, walking back towards the city. Almost at once, a car approaches. It is a taxi and she flags it down. As she gets in, it starts to snow. Snow clouds, the driver says as they move off, hit the warmer air over the city and drop their load. Snow whirls past the black windows and flakes pelt the windscreen, forming icy ridges on the windscreen wipers.

At Hampden Road where Lisa alights, snowflakes spin around violet street lamps. She throws her hood back and lets the flakes settle on her hair, her brows and her lashes. She licks them, melting, from her lips. The snow is crêpey underfoot as she walks through muffled silence, along the streets. Suddenly doors burst open and children dressed in scarves, mittens, beanies and jackets pour out into the snowy street, shouting, throwing snowballs, laughing. Lights from open doors and windows glow on them, and highlight the detail in eaves, corbels and finials on verandas, walls and lamp posts, the patterns thrown into relief. It is as though a roller of white paint has been swept across the landscape, creating a street scene of a European winter, an aberrant dream stolen from another time, another place that will melt before dawn.

Lisa pauses at the corner of her street. She glances along to her cottage, wanting its warm lit windows and snow-clad prettiness to take her by surprise. Instead, she sees a silver Saab parked at the kerb. One of a line of cars, it is losing definition in the blur of snow. Its rear window is filmed over with a cataract whiteness, the side windows are fogged up. Lisa detects a faint glow inside, as though from the tip of a cigarette. James has pursued her, he has tracked her down, he is on the hunt. She is not surprised, for cannot the victim's flight become the predator's lure? But he is in her territory now, hasn't he realised? It is time for the roles to change, for the hunter to become the prey.

Sauntering down the footpath, Lisa turns in at her gate and walks down the path. She fits the key in the lock, and I wait for her to push open the front door. She smiles at me as she comes in. She turns and looks out, and light falls across the snowy garden. I see snow drifting down, and close up, her hair loosening from its knot. Then a car door slams. Footsteps approach. The gate swings open.

These sounds are my cue. Quickly I retreat to the living room and place three crystal glasses and a decanter of port onto a low polished table. The curtains are drawn, the fire blazes, shadows dart above walls lined with books. The room is ready, and outside the snow transforms the darkness into a blank sheet on which the real story of the evening is about to be written.

The Dress

It wasn't any dress I was looking for, but *my* dress; waiting on its hanger cool as a waterfall in a glade, touched by no one, just waiting for me. And all I had to do was find it.

Am I wearing that dress? No!

Did I find that dress? No!

I went from shop to shop; from cheapy fast sales emporiums with dresses lined up all the same like prisoners awaiting sentence to exclusive boutiques that collect rare dresses and pin one out in the window like a beautiful butterfly, exotic and expensive.

I tried some on. Yanked the zips and pulled them about and squeezed my boobs and strutted and smiled…and tugged and grimaced: God! What a torment! Getting my jeans down and my shirt pulled over my head, again and again; no bra and my underarm hair sticking out… Those shop girls, Jesus they sneered, and I felt so hot and ungainly and sort of graceless, you know how those places make you feel. Well, I tried on four dresses.

Did they fit me? No!

Did I find one? No!

Yeah…OK…one did fit…the last I tried on, at that boutique opposite the train station, you know? The Birdcage. It's all hung about with baubles and chiffon and glitter. I found a dress there, and it fitted! Sure it fitted, like a glove… But wow! My dress? If I want to be a lady of the night leaning into the warmth of musky evenings over the canyons of the streets, my hair flowing, calling and singing…a nightingale of the subways…madam joy…

Pale cream with pink sprigs and blooms at the edges, my brown body pushing between the straps rich and ripe, the front split to the waist, tied with pink strings that come undone, slip undone so's a boob, a brown velvet boob, can fall in to anyone's hand like a bird from a tree, warm and soft and tender with a hyper heartbeat and a flutter that sets the cocks standing up… Creamy white with pink embroidery and look! A flouncy frill bouncing around the hem in case you missed the message at the top.

Sure, it fitted, that dress…like a skin, like a dream. But *my* dress? My dress?

The shop assistant…a hard and fast Medusa with marble eyes…she thought she had it made. Suits your skin, she says, fits you so well… just made for you…wear it night or day. And she hitches the straps and lifts my boobs and smooths it over my hips and stomach with tender fingers… Just made for you, she whispers, just made for you she cries…a dream! Oh yeah! Suits my skin…fits me so well…night and day, day and night… And I twirl up and down that little boutique hung with baubles and chiffon and my breasts bounce and the slit slips open and the frill flounces and I laugh and dance and in six mirrors are six of me and six more and I fill that boutique with pink and pale cream in the heady scent of the musky late afternoon…

Behind my back stands that stone-eyed Medusa, ready to pluck my joy and turn it to metal and she smirks at her assistant and gives her the thumbs up… I rip off that dress, the dress that I had longed for, and it hangs lifeless over her arm, and I leave in my jeans and shirt, walking into the clamour of the early evening city… Did I find my dress? Yes! Am I wearing that dress? No! But still, I have my joy.

On the Shore

I told the police, I had nuthin to do with it. If I hadn't of been hangin out with me mates, pissin on last night, I would've got down to the shore earlier, for sure. I surfaced about ten, dunked me head under the cold water tap and went down to check the surf. Waves grumblin across the cliff platform, draggin at kelp bundles, you haveta look where you put your feet, shells can cut 'em to pieces.

'Get to the point, mate,' they said.

'Lighten up! You want the truth? Tellin yer.'

It hadn't looked good, sea fog blottin out the bay, greasy surf rats-arse, waves slidin up the sand, hissin along the shore. Needed an offshore wind to shift the fog, get some surf pumpin.

'See anything at all, anything might help?' one said.

'Heard someone putterin out on the bay, prob'ly a tinny headin out to one of the yachts out there.'

'Who?'

'Don't ask me.'

'A local? Fisherman? Divers?'

'Couldn't tell, no way.'

'What boats were missing?'

'Wouldn't know.'

'You tell us what you know,' they said. 'And fast.'

'I don't know nuthin.'

'Who lives here?'

'Just me and me dad.'

'Your old man is all?'

'Yep.'

'What's he do?'

'Works lookin at things. Studying, you know?'

'Study?'

'Marine stuff. Fish.'

'Poncy nutter, eh?'

'Nah. Not really.'

'Who were you drinkin' with last night?'

'Snapper, Codfish, Koota…'

'You takin' the piss!'

'Me mates. Oh, Birdie turned up later with Chelsea.'

'Woman?'

'Nah, dog.'

That floored 'em.

'Tellin yer, we jammed a bit on our guitars, got pissed, mucked about till late…'

'Your mates, they can confirm this?'

'Check the pile of bottles in the recycling. Couldna drunk them all m'self.'

'Write down names and phone numbers, all of them.'

'Chelsea too?'

'No lip from you, mate.'

They went off for a walk, the two of them. Had a smoke.

Thing is, there was somethin… I dunno… We did races down the cliff path, timing it. Sick! Chelsea was fastest, jokin… Koota made the best time. I reckon I coulda broke the record, I'm so used to goin up and down, but I'd had too much grog.

Anyway, I get down there, gettin dark, few seagulls cryin. I turned to head back, then I heard it, not a cry, more a gasp, as if somebody had hurt themselves, mmt, like that. Hurt, real bad.

'S'goin on?' I yelled.

Everything's still, as if someone is listenin. I start across to check it out but a racket breaks out up top. Chelsea's barkin like crazy, the guys yellin, 'What's goin on!'

I'm up to the cliff top. For shit's sake, Chelsea's treed a possum! They've got the car lights on the tree, Birdie's eggin her on, Koota and Snapper are yellin go go! There's this little possum clingin to its mum, big round eyes starin, scared to death. Koota aims a beer bottle, it thunks right by them.

'Cut it out, you bastards,' I yell, and boot Chelsea a good one.

Well, that's it as far as Birdie's concerned. 'Fuck you, Brady! Kick my dog, you kick me!'

'Have some fuckin respect,' I yell.

Birdie's out of there and the others too, into their cars, doin donuts down the drive to the main road.

Shit, the cops are comin back. Tall one squints at me, short fat one circles.

'Reckon you know somethin'.'

'Nah.'

'Tell us again.'

'Told ya. I come down after ten to check the surf. Fuckin miserable …then I noticed it.'

'Noticed what?' The tall one scruffs me. 'Spit it out before I whang your balls…'

'The gulls,' I yell.

'What about the fuckin' gulls!'

'Fightin over something at the water's edge.'

'What!' The fat one's right in my face.

'Kelp!'

'Kelp and what else?'

'Rubbish. Tossed over from a fishin boat.'

'You're gonna be rubbish you don't spit it out!'

'So I headed back here.'

'Who was here?'

'Me dad…usually…'

They eased off. 'Stuck here with your dad?'

'What are you?'

I took a shudderin breath. 'Here's where I wanna be, go for a surf anytime. I keep a count of the mutton birds breedin in the rookery, right whales travellin north in spring, dolphin pods, always somethin happenin out there…'

'Fuckin Greenie!'

'Greenie dole bludger, eh?' They're circling again.

'Nah, go fishin with Reg, my uncle on the *Lazy May*.'

'Last twenty-four hours, fill us in,' the fat one says.

I give it a go. 'Big swell, storm out at sea, I got some rippers, one monster had three steps on it. One take off, then middle of the face nearly lost it there, one at the bottom. Sick!'

'Stick to the point.'

'Couldn't wait to tell me mates, I rang round, got them over last night, showed them some shots. Rest of the day cleaned and filleted a bucket of trevally put them in the freezer, then trawled the internet until me mates turned up.'

'No one else here, like a woman?'

'Nah, no woman.'

'Where's your mum?'

'Stayin with her sister, Uncle Reg, I go fishin with him, told ya…'

'Right…'

'You're gonna have to make a statement down at the station.'

'Sure.'

'We'll come get you, soon as we've finished down there.'

'Right.'

'Informing you, we'll be takin' a DNA sample.'

'DNA? What for?'

'Evidence,' the tall one said. 'Count you out.'

'Or in,' the fat one said. 'You touched anything down there, we'll nail you.'

I watched as they got into their car and drove off, went back inside and took a swig of Dad's whisky, tryin to calm me nerves.

You see, down on the shore, it was like I said. This mornin, gulls screamin, I sprint through the shallows, yellin, drivin them off. Turn over the bundle and oh shit shit shit! It's a body. A girl! Face white as, black hair like weed over her face, eyes starin. Ooof! I heave away, throw up. Look back, I know that face! Who is she, what am I gonna do? Get back up here to Dad. He's not around, car's gone, where the fuck is he? Gotta do somethin, then I hear the sirens along the road to the beach, and I know they've found her. Then those two dudes turn up, goin door to door. Questionin, questionin…

I'm outa here. Don't say it: if I'm innocent, no worries. But I know how they look for a suspect to get a conviction. If only Dad was here, where the fuck is he, shit I can't get her face outa my mind! See, it's like, she's lookin at me for help… It's doin in my head!

Thing to do, take out the tinny, head off. Stupid? Yeah yeah… Put yourself in my shoes. Get myself outa the picture while they find out what happened. Maybe she was partying on a yacht, fell off, no one noticed her missing? Mates'll come forward, she was with us, went for a swim, we couldn't stop her, tried to hold her back… Or she had a fight with her boyfriend, walks away into the surf, rip catches her, nah, he catches her and then… Oh shit, gotta move! Right, key to the moorings, what the fuck, the tinny's out already? Hang about, the outboard I heard was…Dad? Mobile, outa range! Oh shit no no no this can't be happenin! I gotta find Dad, now!

Refuge

Kate met him at an art gallery opening. He was standing against the wall between the art works as though pinned there. He followed her with his eyes, so she asked his name and stood by him. 'Januscz,' he said. At once they were close, breathing together with no need of talk. The party dwindled, the lights dimmed, the night flooded in.

'Come back to my place,' she said. And he came.

After her mother had died, Kate returned to the family house every afternoon after work. It was in an old suburb of one-storey houses with pitched roofs, red-tiled, set back on lawns bare with disregard. At their house, two flame trees stood for difference, shading the front windows, breaking the heat radiating monotony of red brick. She often sat in the front room where sun through the shades gave a celluloid glow, as of the past.

The past. Who was her mother before she married Don, her father? She flicked through photos of her mother Christine, known as Chrissie when she was young. There she was, dancing at a party, picking fruit in an orchard, close-ups of her laughing with friends. After her marriage to Don, she became Christine and, like him, a Quaker. Their concern was for people, mostly migrants, mostly women and kids trying to settle in, needing shelter. Kate would come home from school and there they'd be, women helping with the cooking, cleaning, hanging washing on the line out the back, babies, kids…

Every evening, her father sang out 'Zippety do da zippety day' as he came in the front door, the fly-wire door banging, his briefcase swinging as he tacked down the hall past bundles of clothes cleaned and mended ready for the charity shop, chatting to whoever appeared in a doorway or came in from the garden, ruffling the hair of whichever child. She gazed from doorways at her dad, the relentless jollity. When was he going to notice only her? Doing good for God forced everything – time, attention, emotions – to revolve around him. She'd rebelled as a teenager. Quietly, nothing overt, mouthing 'Zippety do da' as he came in the door, refusing to take part in the obeisance. University, she left home as soon as she could. Turned her back on her depressed and exhausted mother, and she felt the guilt. But it was her father who'd died first, suddenly. Cancer, and him a non-smoker, non-drinker. He'd confessed on his death bed, to what? An affair, lasting twelve years, a fellow Quaker. Cancer was God's punishment, he believed, and he did still believe.

Her mother changed, avoided the silence of worship at the Friends' meeting house, dread of a far greater silence possessing her, Kate sensed. She became lined and thin, short-tempered, abandoning the charity shop and those in need. Her need was greater, with the loss of her husband, and of her faith. Less than two years later, she died.

A week after her mother's funeral, Kate acted. She got rid of everything, clothes, linen, kitchen gear, furniture, curtains, all of this worn and knocked-about household, and scoured the rooms of the taints of charity, the smell of paucity, scrubbed them from the walls and the floor. She kept only the basics: a mattress she dragged into the front room, with a pillow and light coverlet. She left a couple of chairs and the Formica table in the kitchen. Outside, a wrought-iron garden table with two chairs.

It was to this house that Kate brought Januscz. That first time, wanting to make love, she sensed his East European rectitude, teased a button on his shirt, reached for his belt. He pulled away. She tried again, moving gently, easing off his shirt, exploring his body.

'Are you shy?' she whispered.

Falteringly, they made love and then fell apart, their bodies gleaming with sweat. She got up, went to the windows, snapped up the blind and pushed the window open.

'Come away from there,' Januscz called.

'It's stifling in here.'

A breeze sifted through the flame trees, wafting in late-night scents and sounds, a car passing, a siren like a harbinger.

'Someone is watching, they will see you.'

Sensing unknown dangers in the night, the mental detritus of oppressive regimes, she guessed. His pale eyes were uneasy in the half light, shifting but also demanding when his gaze rested on her. For the acceptance she could give? Anchoring him in time and place?

'See you again?'

Leaving, he nodded, ducking shyly, and Kate took that for a yes.

Evenings, Kate left her mother's house and went back to the weatherboard cottage she'd rented when she'd moved out of home, five years before. She shared it with Sally, a blonde beautician and jogger, fun in a sporty kind of way, never bothered by the big questions. Sally had a married lover who came every few days, stayed an hour or two and left. I've got so much energy! she'd laugh, flashing brown legs and dazzling teeth. Was that it, Kate wondered? A married man every few days? Oh god, not to be bitchy, Sally was okay. She looked at herself in the mirror in Sally's room. Tall and pale, fine hair limply framing her face, she was…what? Plain, not beautiful. Definitely not beautiful. She piled up her hair, slipped on one of Sally's short dresses and posed. It just didn't work. Healthy just about did it, enough to pull an overnight lover. And now she had Januscz.

Afternoons, lying curled beside him on the mattress, Kate heard how he'd fled from protests, uprisings, repression. He also spoke of the saints, tyrants and heroes of his country, and she imagined ancient stone walls, spires, flying buttresses and ramparts. As he talked, his voice was edged with pride, but contempt too, and sorrow. She wondered what he made of this place, a city so glassy and brazen, devouring the edge of an ancient continent.

One Saturday morning at the cottage, Sally asked what her plans were for the house. Sell or rent it out? Kate decided to go over and tidy up the garden, readying it to put onto the market, if she decided that was the way to go. Parking her car under the flame trees, Kate took out shears and secateurs and went inside. In the cool, empty rooms, she imagined possibilities: a new life, escape from librarianship for overseas travel, or further study maybe.

She started on the old aviaries up the back. Grapevines covering them were infested with wasps and fruit fly, paths deep in leaf mould led to her old cubby, where the name Peanuts had faded away. Its musty depths had been her retreat, where she'd created a different family, her teddy Ted, and soft toys, Garfield and Woody, taking the place of brothers and sisters, whom she bossed mercilessly, and she smiled to herself. She clipped back ivy rampaging along the fence and left that in a heap by the path. Already the garden looked better. Pausing for a breather, she thought some more about the future.

Her working day was spent in the Perth Technical College library's technical annex, on St George's Terrace. The solid old building was rare heritage in the strident city. Its white limestone walls blocked out the heat, noise and fumes of traffic, allowing calm and serenity in the book-lined rooms, a refuge for walls of fusty old books on engineering, mining, architecture, metallurgy, geology. She'd loved the calm space, her chats with students, the gifts they brought her – a bucket of lemons, surplus catch from Fremantle, squid, abalone, skipjack. She'd liked the order and routine of handling books, cataloguing them, repairing them, signing them out, returning them to shelves. But what now?

A car pulled up in the street, its door slamming. Kate ran to the front door and let Januscz in. They hugged.

'How are you today?'

'I've been gardening.'

'So now?'

'Let's go down to Steve's.'

'Who is this Steve?'

'A pub by the river.'

'A drink? Good. I am ready for that.'

At Steve's, Kate went inside to the bar, bought a frosty jug of beer and carried it out with two glasses to their table under the trees. Young guys were watching the yacht races out on the river, others sat at the tables, chatting and drinking or calling out to their friends. A couple of families relaxed under the trees, kids haring about, dogs panting in the shade.

'You like this place?'

'I like this place.' Januscz's eyes gleamed. 'This beer too I like very much.'

'Good!' He was going well, she reflected. Becoming more relaxed. More Australian?

'Chuggalug,' she said, and they clinked glasses.

He leaned towards her. 'Kate, why there is no furniture in your house?'

'What furniture?'

'It is stored perhaps?'

'Oh, you mean that house.' What could she say? She didn't want to talk about her mother's death right now.

'What other house?'

Before she could reply, a revving of motorbikes, a gang roared in. Eagle wings and a death head, the club name Pagan Warriors arching across their leather jackets, they swirled their Ducatis and Harley Davidsons in the dust.

'The police should arrest them,' Januscz said. 'In my country they go to jail.'

'Like they wanted to jail you.'

'They are criminals. I was a protester against tyranny.'

'If they break the law, they go to jail. Simple.'

'They are antisocial elements.'

'You're saying that?' She sensed an argument starting and took a mouthful of beer.

'Kate!' Sally bore down on them.

'Hi, Sal.'

'Who's this?'

'Januscz. This is Sally, Januscz.'

'Hello, Sally.'

'Hi. I'm supposed to be meeting Mark.' Her married lover. She looked about the beer garden, hip jutting, brown belly displayed, blonde ponytail swinging.

'Could be inside.'

Sally and Januscz eyed each other.

'How did you meet?'

'At a party,' Kate said, hedging.

'Which party? Was I there?'

'Down at Claremont.'

Januscz swung back on his chair, and Sally edged closer.

'D'you live locally, Jan?' She'd already shortened his name? Breathtaking.

'At Two Rocks,' he said.

'By the ocean? Nice.'

Januscz swallowed the last of his beer. Kate shifted on her seat, her thighs sweating against the plastic, her hands moist around her glass. The gelatinous heat of the afternoon seemed to set firm, trapping them there.

'You go to the bar, yes?' Januscz pushed back his chair.

'Sure.' Sally stood, stretched, pulled her hair out of its band; it cascaded around her shoulders.

'I am coming,' he shrugged.

'Get another jug while you're there.'

He nodded, taking up the empty jug, and followed Sally inside. Kate watched him catch up with her. She leaned back in her chair. So, freedom meant getting off with your new lover's friend, is that how it worked in his country? She watched the bikies, gathered around their bikes, until Januscz came back, carrying the jug of beer.

'A nice girl, yes? Mark, he buys me a beer.'

They drank. They were silent as they drove back to the house.

'You come to Two Rocks now?' The first time he had offered his place.

'Sure. I'll follow you.'

It was a quick drive across the city. Less than an hour later, they turned down a sandy road, towards the beach, where the Indian Ocean rose halfway up the sky. The shack was just that, a three-room fibro structure with a roofed-in porch to keep off the sun. A dense pine on the southern side threw shade, sheltered it from the winds.

Kate parked and followed Januscz inside. The rooms were small, bare, hot. A few belongings, a bed in the tiny bedroom, a table with chairs in the kitchen, cushions on a mattress in a third room. It struck her how little they both had, as if each moved lightly through this heat-stricken landscape. The open doors let in the heat, yet they collapsed together on the bed, tearing off their clothes, pale bodies merging as they made love in the diffuse light. After, they lay still for a while.

'Who first came to this country?' he asked.

'Aborigines. Millennia ago.'

'Europeans, I mean.'

'The Dutch, I think.'

'Who settled here?'

'The English. They came in sailing ships. My forebears, actually.'

'Houses were here for them?'

'No way. Their things were thrown overboard onto the shore.' She imagined sand piling up around the cabriole legs of tables and chairs, ornate dressers stained by salt, chaise longues sliding into the surf, warped pianos tinkling under the burning sun, mingling with the cries of seagulls…

'Huh,' he sniffed. 'They bring nothing?'

'Guns. And disease, death to the Aborigines.'

'Be serious.'

'I am being serious!'

'I am asking you…' That fretful tone.

'You didn't bring much with you, when you came here.'

'My papers only.'

She rested her head on his damp belly. 'Give it time, you'll get your life together.'

'Is not so easy,' he said. 'I am a refugee.'

Drowsy with the heat and lovemaking, she half dozed, thinking reffo, refuge, refugee, fleeing, words chiming through her childhood when she'd thought everyone was a refugee. And maybe they were.

'This Sally, your friend…?'

Kate was instantly wary. 'What about her?'

'This house where we go together. Sally says…'

'Says what?'

'You live some other house, where she too lives.'

Kate stood and walked to the window. 'I do.'

'So what is Sally, a lesbian?'

'What?'

He chuckled. 'I think not.'

'She's my housemate. We share the rent.'

'This other house we go to?'

'My mother's house.' She turned. 'She died. Didn't Sally tell you?'

'The house of a dead woman? It is wrong to take me there and then we have sex.' He got up, pulled on his jeans.

'Januscz, it was two years ago.' She followed him out as he stalked around the side of the shack. There was a lean-to. She looked in.

'I am working now.' Angry. His bare back turned against her.

Littering a bench was a jumble of ironwork. She could make out candles, bookends, a set of scales, firedogs in the shapes of lizards, two-headed dogs, dragons. Forgetting him, she ran her hands over them. Soft, but hard, silky almost, their energy streaming out of them.

In the corner near the open door was a forge, a simple brazier with a gas bottle. Januscz gave it a burst. Flames flickered blue and yellow, almost translucent, charcoal glowed with points of red against the black. He took up a piece with a pair of tongs. The gas hissed, the fire flickered, his body turned, muscles gleaming, his skin catching the glow as he hammered.

'This I am finishing.' A candelabra. Curved arms flared in intricate foliage from the central column which was a mass of mythical animals crawling over each other, beautifully worked.

'Wonderful, Januscz.' She could hardly believe it. So that was what he was doing at the gallery. Exhibiting.

'This I learned,' he said. 'Father, grandfather. You people,' pausing in his hammering, 'you know nothing.'

'At least we're free,' she snapped. 'To meet, talk, think as we like.'

'You do not know freedom. Bikies, gays, feminists, I would put them all in prison.'

That someone could create such beautiful things yet think such violent thoughts.

'They are not good for society, this I know.'

In a temper, she left, and drove back to her mother's house. Out on the front veranda, viewing the street, she calmed down. Such a respectable, law-abiding area, people complained if dead leaves reached the footpath, if cars parked on the registered lawn, if weeds went to seed. Yet a murderer had once terrorised this law-abiding suburb, knocking on doors, shooting the person who answered. But their house had been so vibrant, welcoming, people always coming and going... She wept, the grief for her mother sweeping over her.

Later, when it was cooler, she lay on the single mattress, pulled a light coverlet over herself, and slept.

Sirens sounded. Kate started awake. The roar of motorbikes filled the room. She dashed to the windows and raised the shade. One after the other the Pagan Warriors roared past, police cars pursuing, lights flashing, horns blaring, tearing apart the late-night skin of suburbia. What was happening? Finally, she went back to bed.

Waking late, Kate stirred and got up. She dressed in yesterday's clothes, careless of what she wore to the library. After lunch, one of the students left the daily newspaper on her desk. The word 'Bikies' caught her eye. She unfolded the paper to the front page. 'Rape Police Raid Bikies' read the headline. She skimmed down the column. The bikies had followed a girl to her home, invaded, bashed her boyfriend and gang-raped the girl. Hours of humiliation and violation had followed. Wanting to go to the toilet, they'd given the poor girl a frying pan to urinate in. Oh god, this was happening in her own neighbourhood? She picked up the phone and rang Sally at the cottage. No answer. Edgy, Kate decided she must see Januscz. She left work early and headed out to Two Rocks.

Kate walked around the side of the shack. 'Januscz!'

He came out. 'Kate! Why you are here? I am busy.'

She started lamely. 'The bikies, Januscz, they roared right past my place late last night, the police were after them and look.' She thrust the newspaper at him.

'I hear this on the radio this morning.'

'They attacked a girl, broke into her house, knocked out her boyfriend, and raped her.'

'Because she leads them on.'

'What!

'Like you do, when we first meet.'

'Januscz!' He was accusing her of…what?

'You take me to this house of your dead mother.'

'This poor girl, she could've been anyone. Me, Sally, who knows?'

'Not Sally, she is a nice girl, nice make-up, the nice hair.' He reached and grabbed Kate's hair.

'Get out!' Kate dragged away, her hands to her head. 'What's wrong, what's happened, something's happened.'

'Why you come? I did not ask you to come now.'

'I needed to talk with you.' A sudden revelation. 'Has Sally been here?' Knowing the answer.

He made a grab for her. 'Go!'

Kate dodged backwards. 'So it's all right in your country is it, get off with anyone you get the hots for?'

'She comes to me.'

'You can't say no? What sort of morality is that!'

He lunged at her. She jumped away and stumbled backwards onto the burning sand, back down the shore as he came after her. Retreating, splashing through the foam, she reached the sandbar where the towering ocean tumbled. Diving through to the calm swell beyond the waves, she rose and fell with the monumental surge of the ocean, hair fanning, limbs drifting, tears on her cheeks.

A surge built up. Kate raised her arms and swung her legs down onto the sand bar. Ears filling with the roar of the ocean, she burst upwards as the wave passed over, up through aqua shafts into the air, gasping for breath. Pressing her palms to her eyes, she rose and fell on the swell. Water flooded back, draining from the shore, and on the shining flats there was Januscz, arms on his hips. She glanced over her shoulder; another wave was mounting.

'Januscz! Come on in!' She waved an arm.

He hesitated.

'Come on!'

He splashed through the shallows, hesitated.

She looked back. 'Come on, Januscz!'

The green glassy mass of water rose up, lifted her, thrust her forward, tiers of water cascading as she surged down the front of the wave, and shot in on breakers piling up the beach. She slid across the shallows on her side, her ears, eyes and nose filling with saltwater and sand. Staggering to her feet, she fell and stood again, trying to balance in the shifting, foaming backwash. Splashing up onto the sand, she looked along the beach to where Januscz staggered out of the breaking waves and fell to his knees.

Januscz's Europe? The place had formed him, an artist, a master craftsman. It had also broken him, starving him of a real sense of right and wrong, of tolerance, and empathy. He'd fled in the name of freedom, but clung to an oppressive past like a drowning man to wreckage. Countering Januscz's prejudice and hate would be too hard, like extracting a nerve. Only he could do it, changing in response to this place, this landscape, which wasn't Europe, and never would be.

It was time to be her mother's daughter. She must go, go back to the house, to the safety of a life scaffolded with belief. Because beneath the surface of life lay chaos. Out of chaos came art, creativity, music and stories, beautiful objects, sculpture, yes, and great ideas, science. Also horror: torture, rape, war. And bad ideas. Belief held it at bay, she understood that now. Why not make it a shared house, a refuge as it had always been, for anyone turning up who needed time out, a roof over their head. Her mother Chrissie's house.

Scoured by seawater, washed clean, sandals swinging from her hand, Kate walked back to her car. She got in, buckled on her seat belt, drew back her wet hair and drove away.

Paradise Lost

Holly propped her text of Milton's *Paradise Lost* against a pile of books on the table. The kitchen was dark, though light dazzled at an open window. A puff of air moved the curtains, then the back door burst open, the screen door banging to, and her son Mike ran in.

'Mum! Come and look!' He grabbed her hand and tugged her to the door. 'There's a big parrot up in the trees!'

She pulled away. 'Tell Dad. I'm studying, remember.'

'Mum, come on!'

She followed him into the back garden, into the heat which rolled over her. Mike's twin brother, Dominic, was holding two used cardboard toilet rolls up to his eyes. Holly followed his gaze up into the white gums in the garden next door. She caught a movement. A glimpse of pink among the tufts of leaves. A galah was dipping along a branch, its head cocked clownishly.

'There it is, Mum! Call it!'

'I don't know its name, love.'

'Charlie!' Dominic said.

'Come down, Charlie,' Mike called.

Strutting along the branches, the galah descended, flew over the fence, circled and landed on Holly's outstretched arm. The boys pushed against her, shocks of blond hair falling over their eyes. The galah's crest rose, and she squawked.

'What's this Charlie business, then?'

'Her name, Mum,' the boys chorused.

'It's someone's pet, you know. We'll have to ask around the neighbours.'

The boys faced her. 'No, Mum. We'll look after her.'

'Well...'

'She wants to live with us.' Determined faces were upturned.

Holly carried the bird into the sunroom, placed it on the back of a kitchen chair and quickly shut the door. 'Don't open the door, she'll get out and fly away.'

The boys ran round to the windows and looked in at the galah, tapping the glass to get her attention. Holly returned to the kitchen, shut the door and sat down to study. She shuffled the piles of photocopied handouts beside the open copy of Milton, and struggled with the question that obsessed her: in Paradise, where all were equal, how could there be any basis for discrimination between self and other? Hadn't Eve, in eating the fruit of the tree of the knowledge of good and evil, simply been trying to achieve this distinction, to gain self-knowledge, as well as the power the snake had offered her?

Later, Holly went outside for a breather. She peered over the fence to look into the next-door garden. The neighbour, Mr Feldman, was bent over a hospital bed. In it lay his only son, ill with a brain tumour. The man dabbed at his son's face with a damp cloth, pushing his black hair into spikes around his pale forehead. The white gums, creaking and shifting in the late afternoon breeze from Fremantle, threw twinkling shadows. The man moved slowly, his face tranquil, almost as if, in his care for his son. he was performing a sacred ritual. Tears starting, Holly turned away and went back inside to get tea.

Charlie stayed in the sunroom until the next afternoon. Holly brought home a bird stand she'd found in a junk shop. A galvo pole with a crosspiece and a feed tray, and a fine chain, it stood about a metre high.

'Come on, boys.'

They followed her outside, where she clipped the chain to Charlie's foot and filled the feed tray with birdseed. There was a round metal cup too, and Mike splashed water into it. Charlie seemed to like the stand, strutting along the crosspiece, bobbing up and down. In no time, the chain was tangled around her claws, the feed tray, the water cup and the stand. Patiently, Holly untangled it.

Joe, Holly's husband, came home from work. 'The kids have made a mess in the kitchen getting snacks,' he complained. 'Where's dinner?'

'Last night's casserole, warm it up and make a salad.'

'I've been working hard all day.'

'I've been working hard all day too.'

'Work? Slacking around the university, you mean.'

'The fact that I'm not on a payroll,' she retorted, 'doesn't give me more time to cook and clean.'

Joe went inside, slamming the screen door. Sighing, Holly clipped the chain around Charlie's foot and followed him in.

Much later, the boys fed, showered and put to bed, she sat on the front veranda with Joe, and Ronnie, a prawn fisherman from Exmouth. They moved the amplifier out the window, shifted down to the lawn and listened to classical music. Joe talked about his work in the tax department, insider trading, scams and loopholes, the tedium of desk work.

Ronnie described life prawn fishing. 'Net gets caught up on the keel, free it, Kenny says.'

'Jokin'!'

'Nah. Knife in me teeth, over the side, slash it off, sharks circlin! Scramble back on board.'

'Too dangerous, Ronnie?'

'Nah, lush, every dawn's like the first dawn, the colours, the sounds, birds divin, fish swarmin... Nights on the deck, beer in me hand, sky fulla stars, boards creakin, barnacles clickin on the hull, the lull of the boat... Oh boy, Holly, you'd love it.'

And she would, Holly realised.

Each morning, Mr Feldman left the house next door, briefcase in his hand, to drive into the city. This morning, he saw Holly walking down to the university. He stopped and offered her a lift. She got in, and the old car chugged along, the heater blowing out hot air. He worked in the city, he told her as she surreptitiously wound down the window. Imports, exports...

When she got out at the university, he said with a smile, 'Lovely music you were playing last night.'

Holly spent more time in the garden with Charlie.

'Who's paying for your degree, who's paying the bills, a roof over our heads!' Joe stormed inside as she continued scratching Charlie's chest.

Charlie liked best to fly into the white gums at the end of the Feldmans' garden. She stalked amongst the leaves, peering here and there as though, just back from a holiday, she was checking the condition of her house. She nibbled the gumnuts, holding one in a claw. Bits fell down and the boy in the hospital bed gazed upwards, black eyes shining, as though enjoying the sight of the galah in the trees. Holding tight to her hands, Mike and Dominic waited anxiously for the galah to fly down.

Holly called her softly, 'Charlie, Charlie…' and branch by branch she returned fluttering to the garden, landing on her perch.

Saturday morning, Holly didn't go shopping. Instead she stood around out the back with Charlie on her shoulder, a book in her hands.

Around eleven, Joe wandered outside in his underpants. 'What about the supermarket?' he said. 'Who's going shopping?'

Holly didn't answer. Joe stretched and went back inside.

Saturdays, the Feldmans spent the whole day under the white gums. Their son lay in his hospital bed, gazing upwards. From Europe, it seemed to Holly that Mr and Mrs Feldman had remained European. Mrs Feldman, tall and ivory-skinned, wore dark silk, her hair caught back in a chignon. Holly imagined them as cultured and pre-war, evoking Viennese music, café society and the Orient Express. That which was Australian in them seemed merely superficial for, dominating their lives, was the boy's illness. In caring for him, they had withdrawn into themselves, and now seemed trapped in a foreign country after hostilities had broken out without the papers necessary to leave. If so, it was a calm and tranquil exile they spent there.

'No help around the house, no time for the boys…' On the phone, Holly listed her grievances to a friend. 'No money for clothes, the children's school things, I have to use the kitchen table for studying, after I've cooked dinner, put the boys to bed, washed up and made tomorrow's lunches, then I can study… I'm exhausted!' She listened for a few moments. 'Love? This is love?' she exploded, and hung up.

Love was what was happening next door. Devotion, sacrifice, selfless giving… She sighed. Did love need a fatal illness to reveal itself?

She set up an umbrella on the lawn, spread a rug and sat out of the heat, Charlie on her shoulder. Gazing sideways at the soft breast, pink feathers fanning over plump grey-white down, the scaly-lidded eye blinking, the stubby reptilian tongue, legs as ancient as frangipani stems, as the bird croaked and gently nibbled her ear. Love was so simple.

With the prawn fishing season ending, more fishermen, Ronnie's mates, arrived in Fremantle from Exmouth. Worn out, hair bleached blond, skins burned black, they brought frozen blocks of prawns wrapped in hessian.

Joe was exuberant. 'Tonight,' he announced, 'we'll throw a prawn party.'

While Joe drank on with the fishermen out on the front porch, Holly fed Mike and Dominic and shooed them off to the bathroom to have a shower. Water streamed silkily over their brown bodies and they jumped up and down, splashing their feet and shrieking. She shampooed their hair and rinsed the soap away with a bucket of warm water while they held a face cloth pressed to their eyes. After getting them to bed, she read them a story.

'Are you going to be at the party, Mum?' Mike asked sleepily.

'Oh, in a minute. I'll just stay here with you for a while.'

She lay across the end of the bed and watched the sky darken through the windows, from lavender to deep blue burning with stars. The twins fell asleep and sounds of laughter and music reached Holly.

Joe tapped at the open door. He stood there in the dark. 'Boys asleep?'

'Yes.' She didn't move from the bed.

'Coming, love?'

'I'm coming.' Standing stiffly, she tossed back her hair and left the bedroom.

The fishermen were cooking the prawns in the kitchen and friends clustered around the table. Holly went out to the front porch. Ronnie was talking again about life on the boat. She only half listened as he went on to list the poison fish. Stone fish, puff fish, sea snakes, you go crazy with the pain… But the fish! Exquisite eating, sweetlips, albacore, rose snapper, coral trout, straight from paradise and onto your plate. Spend weeks at sea when the prawns are running, what a life, dazzlin', an existential life, mate.

Existential life.

Hearing Joe's laughter, Holly went through to the kitchen, stood by him, her back to the table piled with French loaves and green salads. The prawns were cooking, tiger prawns, king prawns, the spiky curled shapes sizzled in the pans, the smell of garlic rising. Joe was in his element, drinking, talking, joking with his mates, squeezing a lemon over the cooking prawns, winding a pepper grinder. She tugged at his shirt, trying to get his attention. He lunged for a stubby and knocked her sideways. She fell against the edge of the kitchen table.

He doesn't know I exist,' she said to no one in particular, 'unless he needs me for something.'

Much later, she took a pillow and a rug outside, and lay in a calm and silvery moonlit stillness, agonising over whether to leave Joe, have an affair…what?

She fell asleep with cool air drifting down, woke to the shriek of the dawn chorus. High up in the milky air were clots of mist; tiny birds were flying in groups in and out of the mist. Two and three, singles, on and on they came, a migration. Where were they flying to? When was their moment of being? In the instant she saw them? Before, lost in cloud, after, reaching their destination?

Muffled sounds, the boys waking, playing. Then Joe appeared at the back door, glaring sleepily, hungover, she guessed. The boys came outside and took Charlie off the chain. They sat beside her, chatting as the bird strutted around on the grass. Mike ran inside and brought out two bowls of cornflakes and they fed them to Charlie. A while later, Holly heard the front door slam and the stutter of the Holden starting up as Joe left for work.

'Come on, boys, time for school.' She stood shakily, clipped the chain around Charlie's foot and followed the boys inside. She brushed their hair, straightened their grey school shirts and shorts, threw together a lunch box each, fastened their sandals and shooed them out to the car.

Backing down the drive, Holly braked as an ambulance slowed to a stop outside the Feldmans' house.

'The sick boy's going to hospital,' Mike told Dominic. 'Isn't he, Mum?'

'Maybe…' Holly caught a faint, high sound, like wind in wires, a keening, like a sorrowing, and reversing at speed into the road, she accelerated up the street to the school.

A few days later, she saw Mr Feldman getting into his little black car. 'I'm so sorry…' Holly hesitated. She ached for the Feldmans.

'Thank you, my dear.' The man paused, his hand on the car door handle. 'He had long gone for us, we have long mourned him.'

'I'm sorry.'

'We leave for Melbourne, after. After the funeral… His ashes…'

'Yes,' Holly said quickly.

That night, lying out on the lawn, Holly considered. It might even be a relief, an ending, the chance to start off again, in Melbourne. She dreamed of a flock of galahs whirling above an escarpment scalloping a red landscape. A rent in the escarpment, a shadowed canyon, a black pool edged by white gums, the boy floating in the pool, gazing up as the galahs spiralled down the canyon on a wind keening over the desert.

Ronnie came out in the morning. She was untangling Charlie's chain and the twins were lying on her rug flipping through their books. Ronnie ripped the top off a can and crouched on the grass by her.

'Look, Holly, he's not perfect, I'm not perfect, who is? It's tearin his guts. At least talk to him, you know?'

'Daddy's not going to work today,' Dominic said to Mike.

'Why?'

'He's sick or something.'

'Do we have to go to school, Mum?' The boys were hopeful.

Holly continued unwinding the chain. She put Charlie on the grass. 'Keep an eye on Charlie,' and she went inside.

The bedroom was dark and close. A triangle of sunlight fell onto the red coverlet, and in the glow dust motes floated. Dirty clothes were thrown over the bed end and lay along the carpet towards the door. The wardrobe doors hung open.

Joe looked flushed, bruising shadows around his eyes.

'I'll make you a drink.'

'I want you here.'

She sat on the edge of the bed. He pushed back the sheet for her to get into the warm stale odour of the bed. He pulled her towards him.

'No, Joe.' She resisted.

He wrapped his arm over her and kissed her, his mouth hard on her lips, his hands on her thighs, reaching for her breasts. He licked a palm, pushed her legs apart and moistened her. The back door slammed. Bare feet thudded in the hall.

'The twins!' Holly pulled the sheet over her as they burst into the bedroom.

'Mum! Two blackbirds are fighting Charlie!'

'Call her down. Quick!'

They ran out of the room. She swung her legs out of the bed, but Joe grabbed her, rolled onto her and pushed himself in. He shoved against her again and again and suddenly came, collapsing with a groan.

'Pig!' she spat, rolled off the bed and ran out. 'Boys!'

The twins were out the front, standing on the footpath.

'She's in that garden, Mum.'

'Out the back.'

They pointed to a neighbouring house. Holly took their hands, walked round the back. She looked over the fence. Charlie was lying in a litter of bark and leaves on a rusted iron roof of a lean-to. One wing was spread out and her head was twisted. Tears sprang to Holly's eyes. She climbed on a stump, leaned over and collected up the broken body. She was still warm, her eyes were closed, there was blood around her beak.

Mike started to cry, then Dominic.

'Okay, boys, let's take her back home.'

Scuffing a depression in the hard sand, they buried her under the spreading white gums she'd loved. Mike twisted a little cross out of pop sticks and an elastic band and they stuck it in the ground.

'Bye bye, Charlie…'

'She was good…' Holly choked. 'Wasn't she?'

'Yes, Mum.'

'Race you!'

The boys ran off. To be so resilient! Holly wrapped the chain around the stand, emptied out the water and the feeding cup. She looked over the fence, remembering the boy on his hospital bed, his devoted parents. The house was silent, the garden empty, the trees still, as if all life had departed.

Inside, Joe was sitting at one end of the dining table. He filled two glasses of beer and passed one to her.

'The Feldmans have gone,' she said.

'They've been through hell.'

So he'd noticed? His face was like putty, his eyes red rimmed. He was sorry, she could see that, so how could she say…what? That she was leaving?

'Losing their only son like that…' He coughed, spluttered over the beer. 'Mike and Dom out playing?'

'Out the front.'

'Good kids.'

She knew what he was saying, and her heart ached.

'We're so lucky.'

She nodded, unable to get any words out.

'Take them fishing next weekend. Mate's got a shack down at Geographe Bay.'

'Do what, Joe?'

'Me and you, Hols…'

'Us?' Her voice shook.

'Well, what d'you want?'

What could she say? 'My own space.'

'Your own space.' Throwing her a look, he picked up his beer glass and slouched out to the front veranda.

She leaned on her hands and studied her reflection in the polished table top. Her own room. It would be her passport into realms of knowledge and freedom even though she knew certain knowledge and unlimited freedom were as difficult to attain as a happy marriage. This marriage, anyway.

She grabbed her copy of Milton from the kitchen table. *Paradise Lost*. Wasn't it all about love? Betrayal, yes, but Adam had followed Eve into exile, because he couldn't bear to live without her, even in paradise, according to Milton. Now that was love.

She went out to the sunroom. The fragrance of dry grass and eucalyptus puffed in the open windows, the glare of the sun muted to gold by the slats of the bamboo blinds. Pink and grey feathers from the galah lay curled on the matting. She imagined the room reordered with a table and a chair, maybe a bed. Insulated blinds to block the heat. A retreat? Yes. And she bent to pick up the feathers.

Jodie

The front door slammed shut. Jodie strode down the drive to the car, a beach towel in one hand, car keys in the other. She opened the car door and bent to get in. The front door burst open. Her mother came out.

'Josephine, come back here now. I won't have you talking to me like that. Dumb insolence!'

The girl straightened, swung her long hair back and glared at her mother. 'I'm Jodie now.'

'Where are you off to? It's Robby's car. He won't want you driving it.'

'He won't care.' Robby, her best friend.

'Josephine, listen to me.'

'I'm going for a swim. Right?'

'Dinner is ready. I won't have this from you.'

'I hate Sunday dinner!'

'What's wrong with you? You've changed since going to that university.'

Jodie got into the car, an orange VW Beetle.

'I'll keep your dinner hot, Josephine…'

'Jodie!' she yelled out of the window to her mother, the neighbours, the world. She started the car, backed out and drove away, heading to the beach.

White sky, black water. The heat bore down. Yachts were strung out in the bay. A woman stood in the shallows. Smooth flesh overhung her bikini, and she had the broad hips, Jodie guessed, of having had kids. Sitting up on her towel, she glanced down at her own body. Thin, freckled, bony but strong, that was from her regular swims across the bay. Her solace, the water, the feeling of safety in the rise and fall of the waves. She was scrawny really, except for the smooth bulge of her belly. Eight weeks now. Her baby, John's baby. She glanced up. Storm clouds were piling up. Soon, she'd have to head off, but to where? Not John's flat, a mire of empty longnecks and dirty rugby togs. Nor home, for what was waiting for her there, apart from a hot dinner she couldn't eat? Most nights she stayed up late, listening to Arch McKurdie on the radio, soothed by the cool sounds of Dave Brubeck. In the kitchen, the fluorescent light drained everything of colour and she caught her mother's worried look reflected in night-black windows.

'What's the matter, dear?' Trying to hug her.

'Nothing.' Jodie broke away, retreating to her bedroom.

Waking each morning, she searched herself, longing for the stain of blood on her underpants, helpless, listless, while her mother kept on at her. Why was she so nervy, why wasn't she eating, was it the exams? No, Mum. Exams are over, how many times, just the results to wait for. The results.

She'd caught up with John at a law faculty dance down at the rowing club rooms. Red and green lights lit up the faces of dancers rocking in the middle of the floor. John was in charge of the Kreisler stereogram, and Buddy Holly sang 'It's so easy to fall in love'. It's so easy to fall pregnant, he should've sung. John, taking a break, pushed through the crowd, his big bluff face shining with sweat. He'd handed her a white paper bag, pills to bring on her period. Got them from a mate doing pharmacy, take one of each sort every hour. Someone handed him a beer, and he staggered towards the keg. You could take the whole lot at once, he'd laughed back at her. What, kill herself instead? She'd left, pushing through the crowd, fleeing the noise, the lights, the happy sweaty clamour.

Outside on the jetty, she'd breathed in the cool air. Circles of light reflected in the black surface of the river shattered as the tide flooded in. Couples called out to her to come over, Pinkie and Vickie, Susie and Max, schoolfriends. Once, they'd got drunk together, smoked, threw up in late night car parks outside hotels; climbed over fences to lie on shadowy lawns; sat between the dunes as the moon rose over the river. Now, their talk about travel, further study, sounded so remote to Jodie. She wasn't one of them any more. Wondered, what secrets were they hiding? She thought now, how desperate her female friends sounded at times, not knowing where they stood, ignored or used, hurt by these boyfriends.

There was talk of a new contraceptive. A pill you could take each day, no worries. It seemed like magic, but where could you get it? Didn't you have to have a friendly doctor? Otherwise, it was frangers. They giggled about them, disliked them, were embarrassed by them. What do you use, they asked Jodie. Withdrawal, she said. Wasn't that risky?

After John had given her the pills, she'd ducked into the toilets at university to take them on the hour. Each hour she'd thrown them up. In the end, she'd flushed the rest of the pills away. She and John talked about abortion. Hopeless. They hadn't got the money for the fee. And it was illegal: what if she got caught? So, one evening when John's parents were away, they started on a bottle of Gordon's gin. To the sounds of the Everly Brothers, cooked steak and eggs, and then Jodie ran down the hall to the toilet and spent the next half hour vomiting and crying. When she went back into the hall for her coat, John was still drinking. She got a taxi home, sneaking into her bedroom to avoid her mother.

Jodie turned her head and rested her opposite cheek on the towel. Marriage, to John. Was it an option? Everyone got married in the end, didn't they, so why not now? Just imagine, no more worry about exams, or getting a job, a career. She'd just eat, sleep, tidy up, visit friends, read magazines, until she gave birth. Gave birth!

Did she have a choice? She flopped back on the towel, staring up into the swelling clouds. No abortion meant no to law. If she switched to teaching, she could get a scholarship and study while having the baby. Never. Her mother would never let her forget the disgrace.

Gusts ripped down, twisting along the beach, flinging sand, tearing at towels and newspapers. People jumped up and grabbed their things, running across the esplanade, making for their cars. Jodie snatched up her towel and her car keys. Her hair flattened across her face, she started up the sand. A splash. She looked back. Out on the bay the boats were flying before the squall. A dinghy with a single red sail had gone over. She could see a kid in the water, beside the hull. The woman in the shallows had dived in. She was swimming through the waves towards the dinghy. As Jodie watched, the kid sank, surfaced, grabbing at the upturned hull and sank again.

Jodie dropped her towel and keys. She ran down the sand, plunged through the shallows, diving into the waves, turning her face away from the chop, blowing into the cold dark water. She reached the swamped boat just as the woman dived under. A girl, her sailing gear dragging in the water, clung to the slippery hull, fingers spread wide. She turned a terrified face to Jodie, who grasped her round the waist and supported her, treading water, sank, then heaved up, clutching at the hull, trying to support herself. Above the peaks of the waves, she glimpsed the white cabin of a rescue launch battling towards them. Then the weight of the girl dragged them, her hand sliding down the hull. She tried to grab the girl's arms to free herself, sank, took in a mouthful of water as she came up, choked and sank again. Her head thrown back, she saw, through the film of water, the scudding sky. Hands grasped her head and lifted it clear of the water. The girl stared through dripping hair, her hands still on Jodie's neck.

Together they trod water, but the wake of the rescue launch jostled them. The woman surfaced, holding up a second girl, drenched, white. The launch turned, revved, a man leaned down. Jodie saw his mouth working but couldn't hear his words as, with a heave, the woman pushed the girl up. He hauled her over the edge in cascading water. The woman sank with the effort, and came up spluttering. The launch edged closer and together Jodie and the woman lifted the first girl up and into the man's grasp. The woman hauled herself over the side, water gouting from her body as the man pulled her in. Both disappeared, and then the man was back, leaning over the side, shouting at Jodie, pushed some distance by the wake.

She stared at him, turned away, let herself drift. Rain-laden cloud the colour of a blood blister had closed in, the light purple, livid. Jodie breasted the waves, letting the current carry her. In moments of calm between buffeting waves, she swam towards the shore, coasting in on breakers, slithering in a foaming chute through the shallows. She staggered upright, splashing through the backwash. In the intense stillness, thunder growled, and she bent suddenly with cramp. Another followed, and another. She tried to straighten, stumbled, and crawled up the beach, grabbing her towel and keys, got up the steps and stumbled across the esplanade.

At the car, she fumbled open the door, and slumped inside, gasping. A taste of iron filled her mouth as she fell against the back of the seat. Lightning split the gloom beyond her eyes tight shut. She clutched her belly, broke into a feverish sweat as rain splashed onto the windscreen. Looking down, her wet skin gleamed in the half-light. She pulled the towel around her, stuffed it between her legs; it was bright with blood. What was happening? Blood oozed down her wet thigh. She tried to mop it, wipe it off the upholstery. Robby, dear Robby, what would he say? How could she go home like this? Again, pain, blood gouting, and as she tried to staunch it, could only think of her mother. She was weeping, right now she was weeping.

Jodie tried to push the key into the ignition. Thunder cracked overhead, and she fell back. She took a breath, and reached out again, got the key inserted, turned on the engine. A sudden downpour drummed on the car roof, flooding down the windows, and pain gripped her again. She leaned forward on the steering wheel, got the car into gear and sobbing, backed out of the parking spot. She did a slow U-turn, took another breath, drove straight across the concrete esplanade, veered onto the jetty and plunged into the water.

Road Kill

Roma bored up the highway in her wagon. Climbing out of the Vanaka Valley, her packed bag in the boot, she was heading down the coast to her terrace house, three-storey, unrenovated, one of a street of terraces leaning towards the harbour as if they longed to sink into its purifying waters. Her terrace, where the cockroaches collected at dusk on broken pavement below the balcony where she drank her way through a bottle of wine, wiping from consciousness another day in her public service job.

She'd spent five years at university, getting more than pass marks, and this was the prize? A job as manager of road safety education, working with a team of ex-teachers roving the schools with kits and games, trying to prevent children being squashed on tarmac, skittled on pedestrian crossings, ejected out of cars, thrown off bikes, skateboarding into traffic. The data entry, charts and diagrams, meetings, meetings, memorandums, reports – they wearied her. And where was the man in all this? Nowhere to be seen, since Damon had left a year ago. So. She'd left behind humid life in her unrenovated terrace, and a street where kids and prams and babies and dogs and friends came and went, and the rising odour of rotting vegetation, petrol fumes, rubbish, for a blast of peace, and a breath of fresh air.

The Vanaka Valley, a creation of geological violence more than human habitation. Volcanic eruptions had solidified in basalt outcrops, trapping sandstone in sumptuous cream and orange strata weathering to luscious pink and cream beaches, pile-ups of grey granite boulders, aqua and blue waters lit from below by white quartz sands. The light pooled in hollows, a chiaroscuro giving the valley an exoticism as blatant as a tourist poster. And the strange vanaka palm, endemic to the valley, its scissor fronds like paper strings of dancing dollies rattling insistently, shattering the view as storms surged in. Everyday changes of light, influxes of cloud and wind sprang surprise dispelling the predictable, the humdrum of every day, which, along with its strange beauty, was a magnet to worshipping bushwalkers, holidaymakers' tour groups.

There was little in this place. A disused fish processing plant, marina for yachts and motor launches, fishing boats. A bakery, a convenience store, more inconvenient with its lack of goods, backing the camping grounds and toilet blocks. A single pub, the Vanaka Tavern, holiday shacks, an ecolodge in forest edging the water. As for the locals: holed up in orange kombies with rusted panels rotting in sandy ruts, fibro shacks and makeshift holiday chalets (Horries Crab Hole, Vacancies), hippies and beached grey nomads, ferals squatting like hermit crabs in purloined shells.

What was she doing here? In answer to her pregnant sister's plea to come and stay, stuttered over an intermittent connection. Yep, she was happy to hang out and help out, always.

Maria. When was the first time she'd come to her rescue? Grade one, picked her up after Ronald Pratt had shoved her onto broken asphalt, tearing open her knee. In the street, Roma, fists up, dared anyone to touch her younger sister. Come high school, their mother, fearing for her hapless daughter, had enrolled her in a Catholic girls' school, where Maria had taken to the religion in a big way. Baptism, confirmation, holy communion, mass, the whole sonorous murmuring, stone and stained glass our lady of the sacred heart sacramental, as catching in the throat as incense shebang. Why? Because it was hers, and only hers, Roma guessed. And when she let herself, felt wriggling worms of envy.

But then, Shane. Maria had met him during a church retreat in Vanaka, she said. This coarse no-count fisherman? Hard to believe, but here she was, married, and had been for several years. Still, the old familiar pattern had reasserted itself, the call to Roma for help. So, Roma had hired a weekender owned by friends situated on a cliff above Shane's father's farm, and spent sunny days with her sister, chatting, walking with her along the beaches, cooking her healthy meals, while Shane was away, fishing.

The road wound around the hillside above the township, in and out of gullies where tree ferns crowded, into the shade of a massive macrocarpa pine. Going from dense shadow into sunlight, Roma didn't see the parked utility, its tailgate jutting into the road. She braked, swerved to the shoulder and pulled up on the gravel.

Through the glare on the windscreen, she saw car doors hanging open. At the side of the road, someone was bending, straightening. A woman who stood at the front of the vehicle, retching convulsively. Maria!

For God's sake! Roma opened the car door, jumped down to the tarmac and ran over. 'What's going on?'

Maria's face was filmed with sweat, pale hair limp on lilac hued cheeks.

'I left you resting, not out in this heat, what're you doing here?'

'Shane wanted to check the pots.' Maria choked, wiping her forehead with the back of her hand.

'Look at you. It's too much.'

'Don't worry. You're leaving.' She retched again, her hand to her mouth.

'Hold on.' Roma ran back to the wagon, reached in the cab and brought out a bottle of water. She hurried back to her sister, unscrewing the top as she went. She pushed the bottle into Maria's hand. 'Rinse out your mouth.'

Maria tilted the water into her mouth, swilled, spat and then swallowed.

Roma glanced over at Shane. He'd straightened up. 'What on earth is he doing?'

'Nothing...' Maria gripped her arm.

Blood spattered Shane's white fisherman's boots. A mess of blood and fur smeared the grass and gravel.

'What is that?'

Shane slouched against the ute. 'Wallaby.' He stared Roma in the eye. 'Lyin' on the road,' he drawled, 'vehicle collected it.'

'Shane put it out of its misery.' Maria quivered.

'She said to finish it off,' he said.

Forcing herself, Roma looked closer. Tiny teeth were sprayed on the grass by a gaping jaw. An eye, loose from its socket, looked up at her. Blood was rank in the hot air.

'Gross!' She swallowed.

Shane rocked back on his heels. 'I do what she says.' Eyes light in his weathered fisherman's face, tattooed arms, shaved head.

'Don't blame her!'

'Blamin'? Am I blamin' you, Maria?'

'No, Shane.'

'Let's go, sis.'

'Shane'll take me home.'

Roma took Maria's arm, determined. 'You're coming with me.'

'It couldn't be helped, Ro.' Maria resisted, one hand at her mouth, the other on her stomach.

'Back to my place. Come on.'

'You've closed it up.'

'I can open up. It'll be cooler than your cabin…' Two rooms, with a transportable shower bay and a toilet attached. 'I'll take her home,' she called to Shane.

He lifted the picket. In agreement? Roma didn't bother to find out. She helped Maria into the passenger seat, climbed in and slammed the door. In the rear-vision mirror, she watched Shane drag the slaughtered animal across the gravel shoulder and toss it into the bush below the road. She started the engine. Maria was slumped, her head back against the headrest, eyes closed, her hands clasping the seat belt that strained above her belly.

'Feeling any better?'

'Better? You're the one knows what's better.'

Sighing, here we go again, Roma bit her lip and drove back the way she had come, back to the place she'd just left for good, back into the Vanaka Valley.

At the farmhouse down the hill, Brody was scraping blue metal out of the truck tray and spreading it onto the drive with the edge of a shovel.

'Take a break, Chas,' he called to his mate, stopped to watch Roma's four-wheel drive chugging up the hill, back to the place on the clifftop. What was up? Why was she coming back? Sure to be about Maria. Shane, his useless son, what would he know about caring for a pregnant woman, the blockhead. Up the hill, car doors slammed. He saw Roma dart out of sight and back, then the two women walked across the drive to the house. What the hell did Shane see in Maria? You couldn't get a word out of her, most days. The sister, Roma, a different kettle of fish. A good sort, make a good barmaid. If Shane had got her up the duff instead… Not that she'd touch a fool like him with a barge pole.

Chas turned the engine over. It was running rough. Brody signalled to cut it, lifted the hood, reached in with a dirty rag and pulled the spark plugs one by one. Peered at them, gave them a rub, checked the gap with a dirty nail and stuck them back.

'Take it away,' he called, lifting his hand. The engine started up, fine. 'She's right,' he called.

Chas gave him a salute, and took off down the drive, dust and gravel spinning from the tyres. Brody started to go into the farmhouse to have a quiet whisky. Changed his mind. Wiping his hands on the oily rag, he walked across the yard, through the gate and across the paddock. He started up the hill to check out his daughter-in-law, see how she was faring. It was his grandson she was carrying; he was keeping an eye on her. Tragedy had always been there in the Vanaka Valley, there's no denying it, a lawless place. Whale and seal slaughter, destruction of the scallop beds, Aborigines, his forebears, wiped out… But that was the past, and right now he had a daughter-in-law and a baby to think about.

Maria had tensed as the four-wheel drive left the sealed road and charged up the gravel drive. 'This isn't the way to the cabin.'

'Cool off here,' Roma soothed. 'Shane'll take you back when you're feeling better.'

'He won't like it.'

'Sweetie, I've been here all of three days. Did he like even one minute of it?' Roma parked, jumped out, went across to the front door, found the key hidden under the brass Buddha and opened the door. Returning, she helped her sister out, across the gravel drive and inside, helped her to the sofa, lifted her legs, slipping off her sandals for her, massaging her swollen ankles.

'Now. Orange juice?'

'I can't drink orange juice, you know that…'

'Tea then,' Roma soothed. She heated the jug, her eyes on Maria, stretching an arm beside her head, blonde hair on her brow curled with sweat, a posture so defenceless, Roma's heart ached with that familiar protective pain. She filled a mug of herbal tea, shook it, letting it infuse, placed the mug on a low table. 'Here you go.' Then started. A man appeared at the french doors.

'Maria?'

'Brody, Shane's dad, Roma.'

Roma walked across to push to door further open. 'Come in, ah, Brody.'

'Come to see me daughter-in law.'

'Come in,' Roma repeated.

The man wiped his feet on the mat, though it wasn't wet outside, and stepped inside, bringing in a metallic, oily whiff. Roma had seen Brody in the paddock as she'd driven past, motionless as an Easter Island statue. She'd wave, and he'd make a movement of his hand, that was it.

'Maria. She's feeling the heat,' Roma said.

'No good for her, this weather.' He went over to her.

'Hi, Brody.'

'You okay, girlie?'

'Bit woozy.'

'Here.' Roma offered Maria her drink.

Maria turned her head away.

Brody took the mug from Roma. 'This'll do you good,' he coaxed. He was used to treating sick animals. He eased the mug into Maria's hands.

She took it, and sipped. 'Thanks,' she squeaked, and looked over the rim at Roma, green eyes large.

Roma opened the doors wider.

'It's a scorcher,' Brody said.

'It's too hot in that little cabin they're renting.'

'They'll need somewhere decent to live. Shane hasn't thought it through.'

Shane. Roma sought to divert talk away from him. 'Have a seat. There's a stubby in the fridge.'

'Weren't you headin' off?' The man pulled out a chair and sat at the table.

'Yes. I'll wait a while, till Maria's feeling better.'

'Don't mind me.'

'That's all right, Maria.'

'You havin' one?'

'Yes.' She got two stubbies of beer from the fridge and placed one on the table.

Brody ripped open the stubby and took a long gulp. He shifted on his chair, averting his gaze. 'Maria. She's not, you know…'

'Oh! No, no contractions, are there, Maria? It was just…' and stopped: the road kill, the reek of blood. She gulped the beer and smacked the bottle down on the tabletop.

'James and Sal… They're not comin' back for a while?'

'Not that I know of.' The people who rented her this place.

Brody looked around. A smart place, painted white everywhere, near empty, not his cup of tea. But he felt bloody proud. The land had been useless, edging the cliff. If it gave that pair of yuppies pleasure, well and good, money in his pocket, nuthin' wrong with that.

'This was all my land,' he said. 'Sold it for a packet. Nice view, they said.'

'It's beautiful,' Roma said, looking out at a blue sublimity beyond the brink of the cliff.

'Can't eat the view. If you could shoot the view, I would've, just like any useless animal, an old dog or a clapped out horse. Toss 'em over the cliff.'

'Oh!' Gulping her beer, Roma imagined piled-up skulls, jaws, cradles of ribs played by tides and currents.

'Don't you worry, I got no horses these days. Pain in the arse, always something goin' wrong with them, thank god for the internal combustion engine.'

'Well.' Roma stared at the table, unable to think what to say. The man was impenetrable, gaunt, granite-hard.

'Gotta head back to the city?'

'Yes.'

'Had enough, eh?'

She certainly had. 'I was here for Maria.'

''Bout time someone was.'

'Brody…' Maria whispered.

At once he got up. 'What, darl? Need somethin'?' He bent over her, sheltering the woman almost.

'Roma needs to get back home.'

'I'll hang around a bit.'

'Sure. Brody?'

'Anythin you want, darl.' He nodded at Roma.

She picked her keys up off the table. 'Maria?' Roma went to her side. 'You sure you're feeling better?'

'I'm fine.' She'd broken into a sweat, her hands on her belly.

'You sure? Another drink?'

'No, just go!' Maria collapsed against the sofa back, exhausted.

'I'll see to her, don't you worry.' Brody went to the tap and filled a glass with water. 'Here you go.' Again, he held the glass to her lips, stroked the hair from her sweaty forehead, as she sipped.

Roma looked on, feeling like an intruder.

There was the sound of a car charging up the drive.

'Someone's here.' Roma stopped at the doors.

The ute braked, scattering gravel, pelting it against the windows.

'Oh God, Shane.' Maria tried to get up.

Brody held her.

'He won't like it.'

'Don't you worry,' Brody grunted. 'I can handle Shane.'

The ute door slammed. Roma backed back to the sofa. Boots crunched on gravel.

Shane came through the open doors swinging the star picket smeared with blood and fur. 'You here, meddlin'?'

'Put that fuckin picket down.'

'What rubbish you talkin' now, old man?' Shane stomped forward. 'Messin' with my life.'

'Maria needed to rest,' Roma said. 'She'd had it, Shane.'

'Seein' she's okay, you can all piss off.'

Brody swung round. 'About time you cared for her right.'

'Like you did with Mum?'

Maria tried to get up. 'Not now, Shane.'

'Pneumonia. What was I s'posed to do?'

'Get her to a fuckin' hospital! Any man'd do it.' He turned to Roma. 'She was nuthin' but a fuckin' workhorse for him.'

Brody rubbed his stubble. 'She wouldn't let me. You know that.'

'Fuckin' no doctor stuff, the lord will heal, you coulda ignored it.'

Maria started. 'No, Shaney.'

'Go against her faith?' Brody appealed to Roma.

'She was my mum!'

'Yes, she was, love…' Maria consoled him.

'This is all shit under the bridge…' Brody broke away.

'And Angel? He's shit under the bridge?'

'Who's Angel?' No one answered Roma's question.

'Cut himself loose, more than you ever did!'

'Sellin' off the land did his head in, is why!'

'I made good money out of it, told yer. For the family.'

Shane circled him. 'Money! Give you a fuckin' great hit, eh?'

'Shaney,' Maria wailed.

He looked over at her, shrugged.

'Stop this.'

'Listen to her,' Brody said. 'Listen to your wife.'

Black anger. 'Shut it! Fuckin'…I know what's best for her.'

Roma tried to help Maria up. 'You can't stay…'

The woman pushed her away.

'Where's he dumped, is why I never hear from him?' Shane taunted Brody.

Roma gasped. 'What!'

'You think I'd do that, my own flesh 'n' blood?'

'You? Do anythin' for money.'

'Told yer. He did the right thing, pissin' off.'

'He wouldna gone without sayin'! Not my bro!'

'Sayin' what, you useless piece of shit…'

Shane swung the picket. Missed a vase, hit the side of the bookcase. Books fell.

'That's enough! Stop right now.' Roma stepped between the two men.

'Fuckin' idiot… Settle down, for your wife's sake.' Brody backed out through the doors. He nodded to Roma, lifting his hand, bare head grizzled grey, his back dusty in the sudden glare of heat.

She watched him go. A hard man, forged by this place, but with tender concern for Maria and the unborn baby. She felt a quiver of liking for the old farmer.

Roma turned back into the room. Shane was kneeling, feet bare, calloused, filthy, bloodstained boots thrown awry.

"I lost it. Sorry, sorry, darlin'.' Pleading, hugging Maria, his head in her lap. 'Findin' you here doin' me head in!'

'I just needed to cool down, nothing else.' Stroking his head, the head of the penitent.

'I can't hack it, you know I can't. He gets me goin', every time…'

Maria took Shane's hands, lifted him, for long moments, as the drowning sun sent a last crimson shaft into the white room.

'Roma coughed. 'I'll be off now…'

'Thanks for coming, Roma,' without looking up from Shane.

'Fine.' She dropped the house keys on the table, replaced the books. 'Lock up, put the keys under the pot.'

'We'll do that, eh' Shaney?

'See you in a few weeks. Keep well.'

'Shane'll give you a call.'

'Okay… Bye' love. Shane.'

Neither answered, neither watched her leave.

Roma walked across the gravel and got into the wagon. She breathed deep breaths, started the engine and headed down the drive.

A few minutes later, she was climbing back out of the Vanaka Valley. As she sped round the hillsides, the township simmered below the leaf canopy, the blue bay streaming to a horizon sharp as a garotte. Fleeing back to the city high-rise, to nine to five, a life of work and the rules and regulations imposed to keep everybody safe, free from harm, and whole. The burden of state-regulated safety?

She reached the spot where Shane had finished off the wallaby. A lurch in her stomach, she drew over, thrust open the door and leaned out, choking. Wiped her mouth with the back of her hand, rested her head against the steering wheel. The diamond edge of Maria's faith, she'd seen, was drawn to the Vanaka, the violence of its primal beauty a daily spiritual testing through which she gained grace.

For herself, life was the seemingly carefree cheek-by-jowl living of her row of terraces, with no more to trouble her than daily life in streets overhung with greenery. Not, definitely not, the chaotic anarchy of the valley, its mystery and violence. She would always come to help her sister, but she would be a reluctant visitor, an outsider, a non-believer. She slammed the car door and drove away from the valley where the Vanaka palms clattered their scissor fronds, slicing the landscape to shreds in rising winds.

Palmyra

For the people of Homs, Syria

They came into Homs in the early afternoon. Found a hotel right on the street called, rather grandiosely, Ambassadors. Jacky sent Zara in to the reception desk to do the bargaining. It was run by a couple of young Syrian guys who spoke little English, some French. The tariff was too high, she said, and turned to go. How much then? And dropped the price a pound. She accepted.

November; the weather was cold, she had a bad cough and was blistering, sores as big as her hand around her waist and bra line, exhaustion from too much travel. Train from western India, into Pakistan, Quetta south on a smugglers' train into Iran, then hitching with a Baha'i faith couple, then into Turkey in the front of a transport travelling to Germany, over snowy passes where trucks lay overturned and robbed, through tawny autumn landscapes with villages in the distance pierced with minarets, then south in an empty train into Syria.

A flight across central Asia, stopping at ancient cities and citadels, Fatipur Sikri, Jaiselmer, Persepolis, Mohendo Jaro, and planning to go on to Palmyra. Arriving at towns and villages as night was falling, snow whirling, locals entranced by their sudden appearance, these wealthy Westerners known from movies shown in village halls, invading their imaginations while the wind howled in the blackness outside, and the forests drew nearer.

The patrons showed them their room, introducing themselves as Ahwan and Hassed, effusively wishing them well, and to ask for anything, anything at all. Young guys; regular guys, Americans would call them. Zara asked about bathroom and washing facilities. Ahwan showed her the shower room along the passage, a windowless concrete room, with a water spout high up. There was no hot water and the room was as cold as stone. She was too weary to protest. She asked after a Turkish bath; yes, for men, not women. She would have to make do. Soon, they would have to go out and get food. She wanted to rest first.

Zara stood by the window and looked out. A nondescript place, this Homs, and she wondered where the old quarter of the city was. From her pack, she took out an old travel book she'd picked up at a pavement bookstall in Rawalpindi. She flicked through it, glancing at the photos, stopped at one plate, passing her hand across it as if to remove dust, or a hesitancy of memory, time and place. It was a photo of Palmyra, the ancient city laid out in black and white, avenues of columns, temples to Bel and Baal Shonin, the Temple of Nebo, the Valley of the Tombs in the background, a senate, a theatre. The remains of great days and grandeur. Immersed in it, she didn't hear Jacky call her to the bed.

'Zara, come on…'

She closed the book and went over. He pulled her down, and she fell onto him. He slipped his hands under her blouse, unfastened her jeans and pushed at them.

'Careful,' she winced with the pain of her blisters.

They made love slowly, barely moving. Finished, she thought of the freezing shower room with its single pipe and cold water. She sighed, almost fell asleep, but Jacky got up and dressed. It was time to go out.

Down the stairs to street level, where Ahwan and Hassed introduced them to a man called Abdul Halim, a cousin, who had a *perfumerie* under the hotel. Ranged on glass shelves along mirrored walls were little bottles and phials glowing pink, purple, apricot and gold in the shadowed light from the street. Inside, a delicate scent of almond and rosewater like Turkish delight. They smiled and murmured and Abdul Halim invited them to afternoon tea with his mother sometime. They thanked him, and hurried out to get some food.

At a street stall they bought pita bread stuffed with olives, lettuce, falafel cakes and pickled aubergine. Delicious, and they stuffed on the food as they walked along.

'Zara, Jacky, hey!' Someone called to them from across the street.

Astonished, they stared through the traffic.

A young Syrian dodged across to them. 'Welcome,' he said. 'You are staying at the hotel of my cousins. I am Ali.'

They shook hands.

'Nice to meet you,' they said.

'For what are you looking?' He walked along beside them.

'The Turkish baths,' Jacky said.

'The souk,' Zara said.

He would take Jacky to the baths, but Zara, maybe another time for the souk, when she could be accompanied. Not safe to go alone.

Zara walked back to the hotel just as the muezzins were calling for the five o'clock prayers. Above the plane trees, late sunlight lit the dome of the mosque, and a flock of pigeons, veering around its minarets, fanned across the sky.

She reached the stone front of the Ambassadors, glanced into the window of the *perfumerie,* and Abdul Halim, dark and pale in an immaculate suit, appeared in the doorway. Fragrance puffed into the dark passageway, the shelves of bottles glowed behind him and somewhere was the sound of Arabic music. This, Zara, thought, I could go for.

Ahwan was behind the reception desk at the top of the stairs. 'Jacky is not with you?'

'He's at the Turkish bath. We met Ali. He took him there.'

'Yes! My cousin Ali. He makes the things with wood…'

'Carpenter.'

'Yes, a carpenter.'

'Tell me about your family, Ahwan.'

The family name was Sabai, he said. Very large across Syria and Lebanon, with many properties. Hotels, factories, garages, many properties. A wealthy family? So so, he fluttered his hand. He made her a glass of black tea in the tiny kitchen and gave her a sugar cube to hold between her teeth as she sipped. She dropped the cube straight in and drank the hot tea down quickly.

Back in the room, she lay on the bed and took up the travel book. It told about Zenobia, queen of Palmyra. She acted as regent for her son after her husband's sudden death, and established an empire, an immense crescent stretching from Cairo to Istanbul. Palmyra was the buffer state between the Roman Empire and the Parthians to the east, from where, Zara reflected, they had just travelled. It was the centre of caravan routes linking east and west, and south to Egypt. Merchant-aristocrats made great profits, patronised the arts, built a great city.

Zara lay back on her coverlet, the book slipped from her fingers, and she slept. She awoke when Jacky came in, banging the door and throwing himself on the bed.

'What a bath!' He smelled of soap, hair wet, skin gleaming.

'Was it steamy?'

'Very! A mountain man grabbed me, rubbed me down with this curry comb like a horse. You should've seen the shit peel off. Then the massage, oh boy.'

Jacky hugged her, his head in her lap. 'I sat around the pool with the fellas, wrapped in towels like a Roman senator, took the piss out of an old *haj* about Thai girls.' He looked up at her. 'The guys've got some tucker along the passage for us.' He rolled off the bed and grabbed her backpack, taking out a lacy black mohair top. 'Put this on. It'll turn them on.'

She swung her legs off the bed. 'I don't want to turn them on, I'm filthy, I'm sore.'

'Just give them a buzz. You can do it.'

'Why don't we offer to pay for the food?'

'And insult their hospitality? Anyway, the less we spend, the more we can travel, simple. You know it.'

'I don't want to travel on. Why not stop, rest up for winter, enjoy the culture…'

He clicked his tongue crossly.

'Why not?'

'Possessions, routines, habits, got to keep moving, like the permanent revolution, you know? Or you might as well be back home in Aussie.'

She felt a sudden intense nostalgia for home. Christmas would be coming on, the heat, the beaches, the rush of the easterlies in the white gums, the sky a pure blue arc.

'Not piking on me, are you, Zara?'

She turned away.

'Look, we'll go down to Israel, rest up on a kibbutz for a couple of weeks, okay? It's a cheap option.'

Cheap!

'I want to rest, do some writing. In Greece. I want a Greek island.'

'Don't give me that. It's romantic bullshit.'

Grabbing a towel and a toilet bag, she followed him out and made for the shower. Inside, she flicked on the dim light and locked the door. Taking off her clothes, she dropped them in a corner and turned on the rusty tap. Water fell from high up, spurting over a long stain on the wall. She held out her hands. Water splashed on her palms, onto her breasts and her belly. She winced with the cold but threw the water over herself until she was quite wet, rubbed wet hands through her hair, then turned off the tap. She rubbed herself hard with the towel, dabbing the blisters, they were tender and red but seemed to be healing. She dusted herself with powder and eased her clothes over her damp body. She dabbed her toothbrush with toothpaste and held it under a dribble from the tap. Scrubbed her teeth, spitting out the froth onto the drain in the concrete floor. She shoved everything into her toilet bag, picked up her towel and hurried back to the room. There, she changed into the mohair top, pulled on underclothes and a long blue skirt, long warm socks, brushed her hair out and left, locking the door behind her.

Ahwan and Hassed had set up a room with an open fire. The men were already sitting on thick carpets and embroidered cushions, around a low table. There were bowls of dips, salmon and cream dusted with paprika, ochre almonds and green pistachios, skewers of fish with green and red peppers laid out on trays, mounds of golden pita bread, heaped falafel balls and bowls of black olives. Flames lit their faces as they turned to Zara at the door.

'This is too much. You're too kind!'

They jumped up.

'No no, it is nothing. Come in, come in!' Hassed took her arm and gently urged her into the room.

'Sit here, you will be comfortable.' Ahwan indicated a pile of soft cushions.

She sat down and he fitted a cushion behind her back so she could lean against the wall. Relaxing in the warmth from the fire, she stretched her legs and smiled at Jacky sitting opposite.

Hassed left, but returned almost immediately with Abdul Halim, wearing a long traditional garment with a high collar, holding a short, fat stringed instrument with a bent neck.

'A lute?'

Abdul Halim handed it to her.

She gazed at its exquisite inlaid wood patterning.

'Abdul Halim is a traditional oud player,' Hassed explained.

'Like my father, grandfather, and so on,' Abdul Halim said.

Ali came in, in neat work clothes.

'It's a party!' Zara said. 'Such beautiful food, thank you.'

'A party for you, our guests,' and Jacky laughed with them as they sat around the table.

'Did you enjoy your Turkish bath, my friend?' Ali asked Jacky as he sat by him.

'Ooof, very strong.' Jacky pummelled his arms.

They smacked palms, and laughed.

Again, footsteps sounded in the passage.

'Who is this?' Ahwan asked Hassed.

'Ghazi,' Hassed said, his eyes on the door. 'Hotel guest. He is a sheik.'

An older man, curly grey hair showing beneath his keffiyeh, stooped in the doorway, a cloak hanging from his shoulder. Standing deferentially, they called him in, welcoming him in Arabic. Ali offered him his place. The sheik demurred, but finally sat. Ahwan introduced him to Jacky 'from Australia, and Zara'. He shook hands with Jacky, kissed Zara's hand, murmuring in French too low for her to pick up. Quietly she examined the cloak. A rich burgundy, it was of fine woven cloth, lined with sheepskin. She indicated to Hassed how much she liked it, and he conveyed her words to the sheik, who nodded in calm acknowledgement.

'Zara needs a warm coat,' Jacky said. 'For winter.'

'A coat for winter? We will fix that tomorrow,' Ahwan said. 'Now, eat!'

Each offered her a choice. She dipped pita bread into humus, taramasalata, with falafels, fish and olives. The sheik offered her a bowl of olives, posing an Arab riddle in French, which she managed to understand as 'Our servant is green, her children are born white and then grow black. Who is she?' Trying to think in French, she knew the answer, but couldn't say it. An olive tree! They laughed. Jacky sang an endless, tuneless 'When the Dog Sat on the Tuckerbox' that mystified them. A dog? A food box? Gundagai, is that your language? Much palm slapping, jokes and silly talk after the *arac* was brought out. Her face felt hectic with the heat of the fire, the noise and excitement.

The men leaned closer, slumping, hands on her shoulders, legs. She drew them up, suddenly wary, looked at Jacky, and he eyed her, and, she realised, this was payment. She was payment. She tried to get up, but was held down, and the sheik suddenly spoke in English, heavily accented,

> It is not the ruins
> I mourn
> But my sweet memories.

The boys clapped him respectfully.

A fragment of Blake she'd learned once in school came to her mind.

> O rose, thou art sick
> The invisible worm,
> That flies in the night
> In the howling storm;
> Has found out thy bed
> Of crimson joy
> And his dark secret love
> Does thy life destroy.

Silence. They gazed at her. Did they understand? Then they clapped her politely. Abdul Halim plucked the strings of his oud, a plangent cascade of sounds, trilling on and on… I'm here, she thought, I'm here, at last. But where?

Late, and she got up, thanked Ahwan and Hassed for the evening. She was tired. Unsteady on the soft cushions, she collapsed and they laughed. Hassad kissed her lightly on the cheek, stroked her hair, Ahwan pulled her to him, Abdul Halim kissed her hand, and the sheik murmured '*Bon soir.*' She took it lightly, as they helped her up, her eyes on Jacky.

'You're coming?'

'When the *arac*'s finished.' And she walked out of the room.

Towards morning, Jacky stirred beside her. She tried to stifle her cough, muffling it in the pillow.

'Don't cough.' He was cross. 'Makes your throat worse.'

Holding her breath to suppress the tickle, she waited for him to doze off.

'You were great,' he said suddenly. 'You had them eating out of your hand.'

'What are you saying!'

'They said you're an Arab under the skin, and would they like to get under yours!'

'With my unwashed hair and blistered skin?'

'You're white, Western, blonde.'

'So I'm not an Arab.'

'You fill the role, they fill in the rest with their imaginations.'

She sat up. 'You encourage them!'

'It's a game, Zara, just play it.'

'I like the boys, they're so, so good to us and all you can do…'

'I got a cheap hotel recommended in Damascus out of them.'

'You are disgusting.'

'You can always leave, go your own way, see how far you get.'

'What would you do for free meals then?'

'You'd be the one up shit creek. Quit complaining and lie down. It's bloody cold.'

'We're leaving here tomorrow, for Palmyra.'

'No. Tomorrow we're going shopping, to get you a warm coat. Now put a sock in it. I need sleep.'

Zara moved to the edge of the bed, her damaged skin sensitive against the cold sheet.

A short while later, the muezzins' call to prayer echoed across the city. Jacky swore, but the sound soothed Zara, and she dozed off.

When Zara awoke, Jacky was already up. She watched him dress and leave the room. She was hot now, feverish almost, aching in her bones. She took up the travel book from the floor and read listlessly.

Rome, waging warfare on its northern borders, allowed Zenobia to fill the vacuum, defeating their common enemies. That was, until she minted her own money – the sticking point for the Roman Empire, money. They sent the Roman general Aurelian to bring her down. After a night flight from Palmyra, she lost at Homs. Captured, she was taken to Rome in a triumphal march, displayed in all her jewellery, the prize. Exiled to Tivoli, she remained, with her beauty and brilliant salons, the star.

As Zara read, images of home flickered through her mind. Driving home from her teaching job in the haze of late afternoon sunshine, black cockatoos called above median strips; but longing to leave, leave behind the blandness, the newness, of Perth, the red brick, the lawns and flickering sprinklers. Her mother had pleaded with Zara not to go away, wept. What about her career? Zara had ignored her. She wanted out, and that was it, with barely a backward look.

The door opened and Jacky came in. He sat on the edge of the bed. 'You look flushed. Try and throw that cough.' He drew the coverlet around her shoulders, then drew it down. 'Suits you being ill. Brings out your colours.'

'Christ's sake, get me a cup of tea!' She slumped back.

A few moments later, he was back. 'Ahwan made it. The boys want to come in and see you.'

'Whose idea's this!'

'They like you, they want to help, maybe you need a doctor.'

She was silent, feeling their concern. Who was she afraid of? Certainly not the young men she'd met. No, it was Jacky, and she couldn't stand it any longer. So what lay ahead, flight or fight? Or something else: a leap of the imagination into another reality, a switch to another time and place beyond catastrophe? She drank the hot tea slowly.

'We're going shopping.'

Feeling a little better, she got up, put on a pair of jeans, a skivvy and a red jumper, socks, boots. She brushed her hair and followed him out.

The shop was a concrete space in a new Western-style development behind the hotel. Clothes were hung on racks out on the pavement.

'Coats inside,' Ahwan said.

Zara followed him in. The shop was harshly lit, bleak.

'What would you like?' the shop owner asked in French.

'I'm looking for a warm coat, please,' she said.

Hassed repeated it in Arabic.

Some women were trying on fitted coats in black leather, houndstooth, wool jackets.

'They're smart,' Zara said to Jacky. 'Fifth Avenue Homs.'

The shop owner guided her to a stand of jackets. She shuffled them along on their hangers. Hassed spoke to the shop owner. He disappeared into the back of the shop, and reappeared with a suede and leather jacket with a black Astrakhan collar and deep pockets. She tried it on; it was heavy, but fitted her well.

'This is all second-hand,' she said to Jacky, taking it off. 'Where's it from?' The label had been cut out. 'Definitely European. Get the styling.'

Hassed said, 'Sent for the Palestinian refugees by kind rich Americans.'

Jacky burst out laughing, and slipped enough American dollars to Hassed, who passed them on to the shop owner.

'Here.' Jacky took the jacket and slipped it on her. 'Now you'll be warm.'

She walked into the street, leaving them to laugh and drink tea in the shop. She tried to pick out the entrance to the souk proper. Maybe carpets would be hanging on display.

As she wandered along the street, a car glided to a stop ahead of her. It was a silver Mercedes, and the window rolled down.

'Madam,' the driver said, looking up, 'can I be of help?'

'Oh, hello. I'm looking for the souk,' she said.

He got out, a large handsome man with the weight of authority about him. He wore a grey suit, and a keffiyeh.

'You must not go alone,' he said, and studied her. 'I will accompany you.'

'I'm fine,' she said and looked back: Jacky and the boys had emerged from the shop.

'Hang on!' Jacky called.

Exasperated, she turned back to the man. 'It will be a pleasure,' she said.

'That is your companion?' the man said. 'And you are staying at Ambassadors Hotel?'

'Why, yes…'

'Then you are in good hands with the Sabai family. Enjoy your visit to Homs.' Getting into the car, he drove away.

'Where were you going with that guy?' Jacky demanded when he caught up with her.

'To the souk,' she said, watching the car turn a corner and disappear.

'You'd go off with some sleaze you've never met before?'

'Why not? I went with you when we met in Calcutta.'

'You're crazy!'

'That man is the chief of police!' Hassed said.

'For Homs?'

'For the whole of north Syria. He is a very powerful man.'

'See,' Zara smirked. 'Quite safe.'

Back in the hotel room, Jacky came in as Zara was resting. 'The boys have organised a bath for you.'

'They've what?'

'At Ali's place. He'll take you there. It's all right. He's married.'

Again, the fast walk through Homs' streets, led by Ali, who chatted the whole way. Ali's wife Jamal welcomed her, handing her a bar of soap and a bottle of shampoo. The bath, surrounded by layers of chiffon curtain for privacy, was set up in a single room. It didn't look like a bathroom. They'd done this for her? Jamal showed her the towel, folded over a chair, and handed her a brief cotton dress. Zara indicated no, she didn't need a dress, she had brought clean clothes with her. Jamal looked surprised, turned to Ali. What was this about? She took the dress and when they'd shut the door, she hung it over the back of the chair. Carefully she removed her clothes and examined her sores – not so bad, the bath would help – and lowered herself into the hot water. Relaxed in the heat and steam, she soaped herself, dunked her head and washed her hair. There was a knock at the door.

'You like the hot water?' Ali asked.

'No.' She just wanted to get herself dry and dressed, now. She emerged with wet hair, damp skin, clean clothes.

'Thank you so much, Jamal, Ali. That was wonderful.'

'You drink tea now?'

'Yes, please.'

Jamal brought glasses of boiling tea and little star-shaped biscuits on a tray.

'Thank you so much, you are so kind.' Which of the boys, she wondered, had been so thoughtful as to set up a bath for her? 'Very good tea, very very good bath,' she said, and suddenly knew what the dress was about – to bathe in – and wondered what they thought of her now, this brazen Western woman. But all she saw was kindness.

'Jamal, my wife.' Ali gazed at her fondly. 'So pretty, yes?'

She was. 'Very pretty.'

'Prettier than Hassed's brother's wife.'

'Hassed's brother? I have not met him.'

'Ugly,' Ali said. 'Good name, much money, ugly,' and he and Jamal smiled together.

So, Zara thought, there's benefits in being a lowly carpenter. You get the pretty ones. She stood. Jamal handed over her dirty clothes in a plastic bag. They hugged, kissed cheeks.

'Goodbye, Jamal. Thank you so much.' And she left with Ali.

Back at the hotel, 'The bus leaves at three for Palmyra,' Jacky said. 'We'll have to stay overnight, then head to Damascus.'

They said goodbye to Hassed and Ahwan. The boys were sad.

Abdul Halim stood in the door of his *perfumerie*, as Zara waved a sad goodbye, feeling the inadequacy of their thanks. 'You will come back?'

'Yes,' Zara said, 'I will come back.'

Jacky was peremptory, impatient with farewells. He was on the move, and they walked quickly to the bus station.

There were few other passengers on the bus. Two Bedouin women, one with a baby wrapped in her burnous, sat by the windows. Zara and Jacky sat at the front of the bus, for the view. They travelled through sparse farmland into the desert. The air was cooling and Zara huddled in her new jacket. A low range of bare hills appeared ahead and the bus started to wind around shallow bends, climbing steadily.

Suddenly they rounded a hairpin bend and Palmyra was laid out in a wide valley below them. A panorama of ruins lit by the late afternoon sun, a vista of columns and more columns topped in places by broken pediments and entablature intersecting in colonnades: the skeleton of a city, its bones gold against the green of the oasis and the blue sky, throwing a ghost image of itself in the lengthening shadows across space.

She gasped.

'Worth coming?' Jacky said.

It was. No words could express it.

They alighted at the edge of the ruins.

'The Sanctuary of Bel,' Zara murmured.

Some distance away, were the Monumental Arch and the Street of the Colonnades, and they walked towards them in silence, awed by the faceted, columnar immensity, the massive airiness, shafts of light and pillars of shadow hung with golden motes. Awed by the silence of a fabulous city reduced to a huge arena of ruins, from times whose spirit was the vengeance of the Lord, the fall of the proud, the desolation of the rich and the powerful. The vineyards are trodden down and laid waste, the briars and thorns spring up, houses great and fair shall stand desolate, the Lord shall hiss for flies from Egypt and bees from Assyria, and they shall come, words she remembered from somewhere.

It was like a vast film lot of magnificent facades used and abandoned by a talented crew, a brilliant cast, a constellation circling Queen Zenobia. She made Palmyra's name, put it up in lights then departed, captured by her audience to leave it to a centuries-long run down into desolation and ruin.

'Excusing me?'

They turned. A local man in a dusty suit and collarless shirt limped towards them.

'Oh god. We don't need a guide.'

'Lay off, Zara…'

'I don't like the look of him…'

The man eyed her, his swarthy face blank, eyes burning, looking her up and down like she was already his possession.

'Jacky?' And knew she was to be the card he played to get cheap accommodation. And worse, if this fellow had his way.

'He can show us to the village later.' Jacky held out a friendly hand.

Zara backed away. 'I'll just be over here,' and walked away, trying not to run. She glanced back.

Jacky turned and waved to her. She ignored him, entered the Street of Colonnades, flickering through shadows and sunlight, history and pre-history in this place, the home of the owl and the jackal, the cormorant and the bittern, the viper and the vulture.

A glint of silver between light and shadow. The Mercedes slid beyond the columns, came to a stop. The window wound down, and the police chief beckoned. She walked over, talked for a few minutes, looked towards Jacky. The car U-turned and drew alongside her, the boot opening automatically. She dropped her backpack in.

'Hey!' Jacky broke into a run.

She walked around to the passenger side.

'Zara!'

She got in, slammed the door, smiled at the police chief, and they drove off. Zara sank back into the warmth of the car, relaxing in the comfort and ease, the scent of almonds and rosewater.

'Zara.'

He knew her name. 'Yes?'

'Your hair, your skin. I will bathe you in the milk of asses, I will anoint you with attar of roses, dress you in beautiful garments, jewels, to meet my friends. They are awaiting you.'

Did she hear that? Had he said those words?

'You like my country? Our history? Syrian people?' He smiled at her.

'I do,' she breathed. 'Very much.'

Glancing into the side mirror as they retreated from this magnificent site, the lines of columns approaching, receding, gave an impression of collapse as though they, passing in the car, were the agents of history, not time. In a sense, Jacky was right: you had to stay ahead, or, as Zenobia had found, reality would catch up with you, take you prisoner, parade you in exile, to witness the extreme of the catastrophic imagination, destruction of your homeland. But that wasn't her, and in the air-conditioned comfort of the car, she now knew she wanted the familiar, her mother's hugs, her brother Johnno's teasing, catching up with friends, running into her cousins, sharing laughter, love, gossip. Cooking! A home-cooked meal! She could almost smell a roast fresh from the oven, her mother's baking, the dewy scent of fresh fruit. She wanted the routine, the regular, the predictable, day by day creating her own history, in her own time and place.

'So. What is your destination?' The police chief smiled.

'The airport, Damascus, please.'

'Of course, madame,' he said in French. 'But first, I show you Damascus, my home.'

Consternation. 'Oh, but really, I don't want to bother you…'

'So much to see, I promise you,' he said. 'The souk. Magnificent. You must see the souk, I insist.'

And they turned onto the freeway.

Sisters

From low on the escarpment, the vast salt lake glittered. Bands of grey and lilac, like ancient currents, scored its surface. Underfoot it would crunch like ashes. A lake of ashes.

The sisters, Beth and Julia, got into the car and drove down the escarpment towards the coastal town where Julia lived. Their first time together for ten years, though they'd sent cards, the odd letter, and now emails. Photos of Julia's daughter, Rose, too, as she grew from a newborn to a ten-year old. Now, an invitation to come and stay.

They travelled between hedges of banksia and stands of tuart, past sheep paddocks with borders a charcoal smudge on the horizon. To Beth, the bleached tones and dark masses, the vast swell of the country was forbidding; this is its habit, distinct in shape, colour and tone. She would need time to get to know it before she attempted to represent it. The road unwound, then, on the right, a glimpse of ocean colourful, alive, and she sighed with relief. A pang for her home amongst the green macadamia orchards and rainforest of northern New South Wales gripped her. She gasped.

'Are you okay?'

'Yes, just missing home.'

'You've only just got here!'

A smack down? Beth winced as they turned onto a sandy track. Julia's house was a kit holiday home, standing high off the ground, with glass sliding doors, and a treated pine deck. In the space underneath were stored nets and craypots, tools on shelves, a runabout with an outboard, and a rusty red four-wheel drive.

They got out and went inside.

'Cup of tea?' Julia put on the jug.

Rose came running up the steps, home from school. 'Beth, come see Dad's boat?'

'Let her have her tea,' Julia said.

'No, it's fine.' Beth wanted to see this boat, the *Cyclades*.

Tom, her brother-in-law, was away.

'He's up north,' Julia said, 'working in the mines. Fly in fly out.'

'When would he be flying home?'

'We need the money,' was Julia's answer.

Rose darted out of the door and down the steps. Beth followed, her hips bumping the railing.

Along the esplanade, a fresh sea breeze was in, rollicking through the Norfolk pines. Beth's eyes streamed as she hurried after Rose. This life was so different to her own. How had she and Julia ended up so far apart? Twins. Not identical: Beth blonde and pink-cheeked, chubby, innocent, a sunny child. Julia sallow, clever, tall. The light and the dark of it, some said. The best of friends, their mother retorted. They love to do everything together.

Julia hid from Beth in the attic junk room upstairs.

'Jules!' she called, sliding over old armchairs, finding her sister wedged between a mattress and the wall, reading a book. 'Come and do something!'

'Leave me alone!' Julia lashed out, clawing Beth's arm.

Crying, the girl stumbled downstairs. She crept into the kitchen and took a handful of biscuits from the biscuit tin in the top cupboard and hid in her bedroom stuffing them into her mouth. At the dinner table, Julia dobbed her in, and she was banished to the bedroom. A shared bedroom, another mistake.

No, Beth sighed now, she couldn't tell Rose that story. But what? She'd left school, getting a job as a shop assistant, she couldn't tell her that either. Jules of course sailed through school and university, gaining first class honours. But Beth was the first to get a boyfriend, a small triumph. John was plain with heavy eyebrows and thick black hair. He had a car, something else to crow about, but its passenger door was jammed, and had to be prised open with a screwdriver. She didn't broadcast that fact to the family. He had a job as a technician, a good salary for then. How terribly suburban, Julia had sneered. Not knowing about the sex they had under the pines, on the back seat, anywhere Beth could lure John to fumble and gasp, her bed being out of the question.

But then, Julia was hardly ever home, staying in the library, studying, she said. John knew otherwise. She was hanging around at a student flat he knew about. They'd gone there one Saturday morning when her sister had stayed out all night. Cold light fell through dirty windows. A crow chained to the ashy grate pecked at a crust. Chairs were upturned as if there'd been a fight, and there was a rank smell of booze. Julia was curled in an armchair, a filthy sleeping bag thrown over her.

'Jules.' Beth shook her awake.

She woke with a start. 'Fuck off!' and clawed at Beth. 'Tell Mum to fuck off too.'

She left for Sydney, and rang, saying she was living in King's Cross, had a job as a waitress and wasn't coming back home.

At once, Mother acted, announcing Beth's engagement to John. A white wedding. A reception in the local RSL club. A week's honeymoon on the Gold Coast. Then, back to work at the shop, as if nothing had happened. Months later, Julia wrote, saying she was going to Western Australia with a fisherman. Mother was caustic. Eventually, photos came of Julia with a dark, bearded man, Tom the fisherman. And then, two years later, pictures of a baby, Rose.

Beth missed her sister. Missed their chat, about books, and shoes and boys and hairdos, lipstick and cosmetics, jumpers to knit, op shop clothes to remodel, periods to bemoan. Jules wanted her own look, refusing to be anything but herself. That was what Beth missed most: Jules's heavy-lidded look, the gleam of her eyes beneath dark lashes, the sarcasm, the wit. She missed Jules's style, daring everything, accepting nothing. Their wordless knowing, simultaneous turning of heads, secret laughter, derision, wonder. Jules her twin, her friend, her opposite, her enemy: sisters in the skin. Without her, who was she? You are John's wife, Mother would say if asked. The mother of two fine sons, Robert and Charles. She had no perception of Beth's other life, secret, underground, lived through art classes and subterranean dreams of space and light, shape and colour, weight and force, dreams which didn't include housework, being a wife, or being a mother. Dreams never allowed to surface.

Beth battled the wind down to the end of the jetty. White-capped waves beat against the piles and the boats tossed, *Cyclades*, the thirty-foot fishing boat, with them.

'Eva?' Rose yelled.

'Who's Eva?'

'She lives on the boat while Dad's away.'

'No one seems to be there, darling.'

As they walked away down the jetty, Rose huddled against her.

'Is Nan sick?'

'No, she's just old, darling.'

'How old?'

'She's sixty now.'

'What was Nan's name when she was a little girl?'

'Rose, darling. You were named after her.'

The girl skipped with delight. 'Nan's name is my name, Rose.'

'Would you like to see your Nan?'

'Yes! Where does she live?'

'Newcastle. New South Wales.' In the same dark brick terrace where they'd grown up.

'Can we catch the train and go see her?'

'Oh, I don't know. Let's wait and see.'

'Look!' Rose pointed down where green glassy water poured through the piles.

Five fingerlings, a handspan of them, wavered in the current, gazing upwards as if seeing them, with their black pinpoint eyes.

Entranced, Beth leaned over. 'What are they?'

'Baby squid!'

With a flick, they were gone.

As they left the jetty, two men trudged towards them. Twins, Beth saw immediately. Buckets swung in left hands, fishing rods poked above right shoulders. Squat in identical old boiler suits and woollen beanies pulled down to their eyebrows, their weather-beaten faces were stretched tight like red rubber masks.

'Hi, Doug. Hi, Bert!'

They smiled and grunted as Rose danced around them.

'My Auntie Beth.' Rose grabbed her hand, showing her off.

'Hi, Doug. Hi Bert,' Beth greeted them.

They smiled, ducking their heads shyly.

'Goin fishin', Arnie Bet, Arnie Bet.'

'Good luck!'

The men trudged off. Was this what Jules had feared, the freakishness of being a twin? Is that how she'd seen it, the loss of identity, the immediate classifying as both different and the same?

They crossed the esplanade. A broken neon sign over a shop said 'Beryl's Eats'. A man pushed his way through the broken fly wire door as they walked past.

'Hi, Eddie,' Rose said. 'This is my Auntie Beth.'

'Hello, Auntie Beth.'

'Hello, uh, Eddie.

'Visitin' for long?'

'A week,' Beth said. 'The school holidays start tomorrow.'

Eddie tousled Rose's hair. 'See you over at your mum's.'

They passed holiday shacks thrown together out of fibro, trellis, perspex. Hydrangeas bloomed beside rotting tank stands. A good wind would blow them away, yet they all had name plates tacked to them. Kwitlookin, Bellyacres, Avagrog.

'Who lives in them?' she asked Rose.

'Miners. They come down from the goldfields.'

'How often?'

'Every year.'

A migration across the brown landscape, like cicadas that, having spent seventeen years underground, emerge for one day of light and song at the coast. And herself? When was her moment to emerge into light and song to be?

'Hi, Mum!' Rose ran to the steps up to the deck.

Julia was gazing out as the girl clutched her. Was she thinking, dreaming, or what? Beth didn't have a clue any more what was going on in her sister's head. She remembered, as she walked to the steps, her sister describing in a letter a fishing trip with Tom, to the edge of the continental shelf. *Cyclades* rising and falling with the swelling ocean in blackness dazzling with starlight so bright she thought she would fall up into the night. An image she now longed to remind her.

'We're back!' Beth trudged up the steps after the girl, and inside.

'Like the bay?'

'Yes, funny little place.'

'It's my choice,' Julia snapped.

'I know that...' Beth subsided.

'Anyway,' Julia leaned at the kitchen door. 'I do go up to Perth.'

'With Tom?'

'Sometimes. For my PhD research.'

'PhD?'

'You know I'm doing my doctorate? Murdoch University. I said in the letter.'

'It didn't sink in. What about Rose, does she go with you?'

'Eva on the boat usually moves in and babysits.'

'Eva?'

'Eddie looks in too, makes sure she's fed properly, not that Eva won't.'

'She needs her mother and father, not a collection of strays!'

Jules gave her a look. 'You sound just like Mum.'

'Maybe she's right for once.'

The jug boiled.

Beth clattered the mugs and tipped the boiling water onto teabags.

'Rose needs to see her grandmother.'

'So that's why you're here.'

'She asked after her.'

'Prompted by you.'

'No, Jules.'

'What, don't tell me, after ten years of nothing?' Julia swung around the room, occupying it, leaving no room for doubt. 'No cards, no calls, no presents, not even for Rose. '

'I wrote to you.'

'Not Mum, though,' she snapped.

'I showed her your photos… What about you! Not the slightest bit interested in me, or my life, my boys.'

Julia raised her hands. 'There you go then. Mutual.'

Beth spilled tea onto the bench, grabbed a cloth and mopped it up. 'You were always the one. I was only good enough to marry the first idiot earning a steady income to come along.'

'John?'

'Exactly how it was.' Gasping at her own disloyalty.

'It was your choice, so stop whingeing,' turning her back on her sister, and on her betrayal of her husband.

There was a tap at the french doors. Eddie leaned in.

Rose ran to him. 'Eddie!' She hugged him. 'Mummy and Beth are having a fight.'

'Tea, Eddie?' Beth managed to ask.

'Too right. Bet you two were best mates growin' up.' He smiled at them both.

Her anger eased. Why did this have to happen?

'Milk?'

'Straight black,' Eddie said. 'My usual.'

'Beth was so good at things,' Julia's voice was almost soft.

'Me?' Beth shifted to look at her.

'She could make anything and look good. That jumper you knitted that time.'

'Which jumper?'

'Light blue and dark blue bands, with a boat collar and dropped sleeves.'

'Oh that.'

'I pinched it off you.'

'I'd've given it to you, if you'd asked.'

'Ask? When did I ever ask.' Wilful, their mother used to say. Headstrong. 'I was such a bitch.'

'And I was such a sook!'

They laughed together.

'Got a message,' Eddie interrupted. 'From Eva.'

'Catch her on the boat?' Julia asked Beth.

'Eva wasn't there, Mummy,' Rose said.

'She's headed off,' Eddie said.

'Oh, what!' Julia went to the sink, threw her mug in with a clatter. 'You know what she's like.'

'She promised. I'm going up to Perth in a couple of days.'

'Perth?' Beth joined her sister. 'Why?'

'I told you. My PhD, mid-year meeting with my supervisor.'

'How long for?'

'Five days.'

'Nearly a week! What am I supposed to do, go home and come back?'

'Maybe, well, you could stay.'

'Babysit? Don't even think it!'

'I'm not a baby!' Rose wailed.

'You're a piglet.' Eddie ruffled her hair.

'I thought I had Eva teed up.'

'So now, how convenient, me.'

'Here you go again!' Julia thrust fists down by her side and glared at Beth.

'I've had it.' Beth headed to the french doors, stamped down the steps, dived under the house. Climbed into the four-wheel drive, and slammed the door. She wouldn't put up with it, like the weak sister from the past. The hanger-on. The victim. It was a mistake, this visit, thinking everything would've changed. She lowered her head on the steering wheel and thought of home, John and the boys. What to do now?

A tap at the driver's window.

Eddie went round and opened the passenger door. 'You okay?'

'Sort of, Eddie.'

'She was real excited about you coming, Beth.'

'I don't think so.'

'Tellin' you. All these stories she told Rose, about growing up, what you got up to.'

'Julia did?'

'For sure.'

'But she's going to Perth, Eddie!'

'Yeah, well…it's for Tom.'

'What're you saying?'

'She's gotta go…' His voice trailed away.

'You mean…has Tom left her?'

'Was he ever with her?' Eddie looked down.

'Tell me?'

'Tom's my brother, he just never settles, one scheme after the other.'

'The fishing boat?'

'Hard to make a livin'.'

'Mum was right, a waster.'

'No shit, he's different, is all, like you and Julia. Still my bro in the skin.'

'Sorry,' Beth conceded. 'Still. She can't use people like this. Me,' she added.

'What choice has she got?'

'To come back east with me, that's a choice.'

'No, no it isn't. You know that, Beth.'

She felt like she'd stubbed her toe on a massive rock. 'I'm family, Eddie.'

'Yep. Like me.' He got out of the car.

Beth lay back against the seat. Family? This place? What was here, the shacks, the pines, the boats, the people... Still, their home, and she sighed. She got out, and followed Eddie up the steps. Inside, Rose was running around with a scrabble board, looking for the bag of tiles. Julia looked from Beth to Eddie. She knows I know, Beth saw.

'Ummm...' she started to say.

'It's carbonara tonight,' Julia interrupted. She wasn't going to let Beth get a word in.

'I can help with that.' Beth stood there, hands hanging.

'No need.' Julia turned away. 'Have a glass of wine.'

'I'll keep an eye on the boat, and this place, no worries, Jules,' Eddie tried.

What to do about Rose? Hung in the air.

'Like I said...' Beth started.

'Like I said...' Julia said at the same time.

Silence, then they exploded with laughter.

Eddie looked puzzled, and once again she and Julia were in their secret world of knowing.

'While I'm here, Jules, it's fine, I'll stay.' Beth cuddled Rose. 'Would you like to come back east with me for a little while one day?'

Julia watched.

'Can I, Mum?'

'Stay with me, and Charlie and Robert? Your cousins.'

Rose gazed at her mother. 'I want to see Nan.'

'Maybe... Next school holidays.'

'Ah.'

The tension eased.

Julia said, 'Christmas, bring the boys over. Plenty of room. They'd like fishing, diving...'

'They'd like that,' Beth said.

'Fine. I'm headin' off.' Eddie walked to the doors. 'Let me know when you're goin', Jules.'

Beth followed Eddie out, and watched him walk into the darkness of night. Far off, the salt lake would be glimmering in moonlight. She would paint him black against silvery white. And Julia? She would paint her standing on the deck, looking into this strange and distant landscape, waiting for Tom, her man. She looked inside, into the lit room. She could allow herself a little gloating, for she had her home, family, secure and solid, in a beautiful place. But that wasn't her way, to gloat. Inside, her sister was making carbonara, and her niece was at the table, placing tiles on the Scrabble board. She went in, pulled out a chair, and joined them.

Truth

The wild swans were calling this morning. A mournful maw maw penetrating the fog beyond the windows, beyond the whirls and spirals of the lace curtains so flimsy against the white world outside. A jerry, the river fog, had billowed down, enveloping the city, all the way downriver.

Marion sat on the bed and pulled on her stockings. Mother would be awake, disturbed by the birds on the lagoon; they always upset her. Hot tea and toast would settle her down. Standing, she straightened her warm woollen skirt, pulled tight her cardigan and stepped into solid black shoes, just like the shoes she'd worn to school. How come she was still stuck with them? There she was in the mirror, a quiet grey-haired woman in her sensible clothes looking much older than she was, barely past forty-five. She turned away from the mirror, clutching her throat. She'd need a scarf today, the scarlet wool perhaps.

Walking down the hall past empty rooms to the kitchen, the cold struck upwards. Marion put on the jug and popped sliced bread into the toaster. Mother didn't like it, but it was convenient; so much was, these days. Hours, days, years of her life had been spent in jam making, bottling, preserving. Decades gone into making bread, scones, cakes, pies, crumbles, tarts and biscuits. Farm life, how everyone had eaten back then! Well, it wasn't for her. She ate like a sparrow.

Marion placed the cup of tea and the toast onto a tray with a picture of Buckingham Palace and straightened the crocheted tray cloth. How wonderful it would be to have breakfast brought to her in bed, with a rose from the garden, all dewy, pink and soft. And who was there to bring it? Exactly no one. She snapped her lips and marched down to her mother's bedroom. She must hurry; it was her day off and she had the ferry to catch.

Mother's room was small but pretty. Marion congratulated herself on it as she pushed open the door. Walls papered in lilac sprigged with flowers, photographs and old china on the cedar chiffonier, a warm carpet, thick curtains. No one could accuse her of neglecting her duty to her bedridden mother.

'Good morning, Mother.' She placed the tray on a low table and pulled back the curtains.

Outside, the fog thinned around gaunt trees to let the pallid sun appear. A sliver of silver glinted on the lagoon.

'Bitter this morning, Mother. A jerry.' Marion crossed to the bed, plumped her up, pushed a pillow behind her head and placed her hands decoratively on the coverlet, then took the breakfast tray over to her.

The old lady followed her movements with stone-grey eyes, her powder puff face blank.

'Are you warm enough?'

Not talking again, just because it was Friday, Marion's day off. Has she remembered what else today marks? Of course. She wouldn't forget dear Father's birthday.

Marion manoeuvred the stainless steel stand with the tray beneath her mother's chin, tidied back wisps of hair and tilted the tea to her lips. Father had gone years ago, and Mother had lingered on, forcing Marion to stay at home, allowing her brothers to do what they wanted with the farm. Now look at the mess they'd made of the place. Dead apple and apricot orchards, degraded paddocks, erosion. Both boys in real estate in town, and they'd been quick to sell most of the farm off for a subdivision, leaving her stranded on a few acres with the old lady.

'Sixteenth of June!' Marion chirruped, and followed her mother's gaze to the silver-framed photograph on the chiffonier.

There was Father as the local mayor, smart in a suit, his hair slicked back, looking stern and handsome. Other photos too, of Father busy about the farm, life of the party, dinner host to well known locals…

The old lady choked on her toast, tears moistening the lines of her cheeks.

'What's this nonsense!'

The old lady trembled, clenched her hands with the effort of control.

'That's better. Now, eat your toast. I've the ferry to catch. Nurse Narelle will be along soon. I'll put on the radio.'

Cheerful music burst out as Marion tucked up the old lady, and took out the tray with the half-eaten toast, shutting the bedroom door to keep in the warmth. After a few minutes, she returned with a silver-backed hairbrush and a face cloth. She worked away at the crumpled face, dabbed it dry and brushed back the sparse hairs over the pink scalp.

'Well.' Marion kissed her mother on the forehead, noting the eyes obstinately closed. 'Time to go. I'll bring you back a treat.' A Boston bun would do.

In the hall, Marion tucked the scarf into her collar, pulled on her grey coat, clasped her bag which contained her purse, gloves and library books, and stepped out of the front door, down the steps and into the fog.

Free at last! Marion's breath fumed in the air as she pulled on her gloves. She walked along the gravel track to the gate where geraniums bloomed in the grass like drops of blood. A catalogue was curled in the damp and with a click of her tongue she picked it up; so much rubbish blew down from the subdivision. She glanced at it as she unhooked the gate and swung it open. Holidays in Queensland. Blue sky, sunny shots of tanned people leaping after a ball, stretching out by a pool, drinking cocktails, what nonsense! She was about to walk through, then hesitated. Nurse Narelle would be along soon in her car; she would appreciate an open gate. So much for that! With quiet glee, Marion slammed it shut and fastened it, stuffed the catalogue in her bag, and headed towards the jetty. Gravel crunched underfoot as she passed rough timbered apple sheds, black with damp. They slumped against broken fences, the wires between the rotten posts strung with drops. Silvered paddocks swept beyond the road to the point, a jumble of boulders at the water. On one side was the lagoon; on the other, the bay. The gravel road crossed the point to meet, at the jetty, the asphalt road from the subdivision. She knew hardly anyone from the houses over there, and none were waiting this freezing morning. They preferred to take their cars to town. Peg Poulter was there, that's all, a scarf over her grey hair, a string bag in her hand.

'Good morning, Peg.'

For years, the woman had given her mother a hand with the washing and ironing. She nodded and looked away. Almost as if, Marion realised with a shock, she had no wish to speak to her. Well! Some people!

She handed Ern, who'd worked on the ferry since she was a child, her fare.

He was eating a brown bread roll, his brown cheeks swelling as he gave her a ticket. He swallowed. 'Off to town for a bit of shopping?' Knowing Marion made the trip every Friday. 'How's your mother keepin'?'

'As well as can be expected,' Marion replied. 'She's an old lady now. And yourself?'

Ern shrugged and bit into his bread roll. Marion smiled her sympathy and made for her usual seat, come rain or shine. A bit of fog wasn't going to deter her from sitting outside in the stern. A few people came on board and dashed into the cabin. A few minutes later, the rope was unwound from the bollard and thrown on board by Jock, Ern's offsider, and the ferry chugged out into the bay. The shoreline receded into the fog, features lost definition, and the familiar point became a dark stretch of land, silver at bay and lagoon, where swans rose with a clatter of wings, flashes of white.

Once, one spring morning, a light mist tinted pink by the rising sun had bellied downriver. Unfurling like a bolt of silk, a man standing by her at the rails had said, 'Voluptuous, so voluptuous.' She'd felt a shiver of desire at his words as they stood together. Looked out for him next time she'd caught the ferry, but no such luck.

Desire. She'd once been consumed by desire. For James. Friends of cousins, he'd arrived from the mainland. He'd liked the work in their orchards, and had stayed on. In their spare time, he and Marion had ridden horses over the headland to the rocky shore, where they picked mussels and cooked them on the beach, squeezing lemons, the juices running down their chins. On black nights, they went flounder fishing on the lagoon with prongs and a lamp, laughing as the dinghy rocked with their lunges to spear the fish. They danced all night at community dances and made love beneath the trees in the orchard, above them the round fruit glistening in the moonlight.

They announced their engagement. James returned to the family cattle station in north-west Western Australia. Marion planned to join him there, but Mother took to her bed. I won't have it, she said. She would die if Marion left. Marion appealed to her father for support, but none came. She wrote James a terse, formal note breaking off the engagement, hoping against hope that he would reply, even return to claim her. She heard nothing, so what was in it anyway? Not the love she felt, clearly. Life went on. Mother had good days and bad days. Who knew what was wrong? The specialists certainly didn't. She never really left the sick bed again.

Father was killed in a tractor accident. How? No one knew, and suspicion swirled. After all, it was a Poulter boy who'd found him pinned beneath it. A wild mob the Poulters, but they'd never given trouble before, why now? Ridiculous. Her brothers took over the property and at once it was on the skids. They wouldn't take her advice to diversify, oh no, content with running it into the ground, then subdividing and selling off parcels of land. Occasionally they rang and asked after their mother, visited even, always with plans and schemes about what to do with her. Marion refused their suggestion of putting the old lady into a nursing home. They weren't going to get rid of her and sell the farmhouse. Did they think she was stupid?

The ferry cut across pewter water, casting silver streamers of wake. Islands and promontories floated in the fog, familiar but remote, morose as half-remembered dreams. Ahead, the Mountain should be in view, but only a tracery of grey on white, ridge and scarp could be discerned. The ferry's engine beat on, and slowly they drew in to the far shore. In the distance appeared concrete sheds, stone warehouses and a line of bare trees, then the city high-rise, obscured by the hummocking fog.

Marion drew her coat about her, tightened her scarf, ready to disembark. A sudden movement beside her. Peg Poulter had been out there all along. Her string bag fell to the deck, the contents of her purse spilling out. Marion stooped to gather the coins in her gloved fingers and give them back to Peg, who pushed them into her purse. She grasped Marion's sleeve. She reared away from the coarse grey skin, the tangles of hair under the rag of a scarf held by two bobby pins, the weepy eyes.

'I reckon it's time you saw this.' Peg pushed an envelope into Marion's hand, and was off, hurrying to the front of the ferry as they glided into the wharves.

Marion looked after her, astonished, then down at the grubby envelope. She thrust it into her bag and looked back the way they'd come, as if searching the past for meaning. The Poulters lived in a weatherboard cottage up the road from the farm. Charlie Poulter and his kids worked on the farm fruit picking, pruning the trees, feeding the pigs, odd jobs, with Peg helping in the house, yet... Ern coughed. Marion started, stepped down the gangplank and onto the wharf, putting unsettling thoughts out of her mind.

Her routine was to walk up to the library, change her books, browse through the shelves and take out her new books. Then, she'd shop for some small necessities, have lunch, a hot cocoa and a sandwich. More window shopping, then a walk back to Franklin Square to sit under the trees until it was time to catch the ferry home. But the streets were freezing. Her stride faltered, she felt a tight anxiety in her chest and opened the top button of her coat. Reaching the library, she sat on the low stone wall by the street to get her breath as people hurried past her. Once inside, they relaxed, loosened their coats and scarves, and smiled in the warmth, as though in another country of milder latitudes to which she, Marion, deserved no entry.

Hesitantly, she took Peg Poulter's envelope out of her bag. She stared at it, then opened it. A photograph fell out, that was all. She picked it up with gloved fingers. It was a small photograph, black and white, of her father. Puzzled, she turned it over, but nothing was written on the back. Who had taken it, and where? It couldn't have been long before he died; she recognised the suit. Beer glass in his hand, he was laughing to someone off to the side of a room. Who, and what room? That old dresser behind him, she recognised that! The china dogs, the plates. It was Peg Poulter's place. What was he doing there? A memory surfaced, of waking one night to her mother screaming I know where you've been – at Peg Poulter's. You dare to come home from her bed! A door slammed. A terrible silence had stretched through the night to a disbelieving dawn. And then forgetfulness.

Marion held the photo away from her with horror. She shoved her books through the slot for late returns, and then the photograph, as if ridding herself of the past and all it had ever meant to her. Blindly, she staggered away down the street. Head down, she reached an area of warehouses and makeshift offices, faded hoardings and stretches of broken asphalt where cars were parked randomly, as if abandoned.

Passing an empty showroom window, Marion saw herself reflected against the black of the road and the white of the sky. A slight figure at one end of an empty stretch of glass. A neat grey coat, sensible black shoes, the only colour the red woolly scarf at her neck. A dead-white face, blank, incapable of despair. What had brought her to this point in her life?

A semi-trailer inched along the roadway behind her, its reflection filling the showroom window, a bulwark with the letters S and D stencilled on the tarpaulin cover. It stopped and began to back, the engine revving, stopping, grating forwards, then backing down a laneway. Exhaust billowed around her. She choked on the diesoline fumes, the plate glass window shuddered with the vibrations, and her reflection fragmented.

Clutching the scarf at her throat, Marion darted away. As she approached Franklin Square, the sun broke through the fog, a stain seeping along the grey planes, deepening to red. The red of blood, of sacrifice, of betrayal, of whom but herself, and Mother. Betrayal of their right to live a good life, a happy life of their own choosing. Tears stung her eyes.

At the ferry, Ern greeted her as she handed him her ticket. 'Jerry's liftin',' he said. 'Done your shoppin'?'

She ignored him, stepped down the gangplank and into the cabin for the journey home. When she was comfortable, with her coat tucked under her legs, she took the catalogue from her bag, glanced at happy people, bright sunshine, blue sky. It was a message.

A nursing home for Mother? Remove her from that poisonous room, those pictures, the reminders of her betrayal that Marion, inadvertently, yes, had rubbed in every day, for years. The boys were right: she should have proper love and care for her remaining years. A sudden thought, and Marion gasped, bent over the pain in her stomach. They'd known all along about Peg Poulter and their father's death. That was why they were so keen to sell the house, carve up the property, be rid of it. She gripped her gloved hands together to control the shudders. They knew. Why hadn't they told her? They'd condemned her and her mother to a frozen life devoid of love. Marion stood, stumbled out to the deck and gripped the rail. Well, she could act. Cut her roots, shake off the contaminated soil of this place, buy a vehicle and head north, north west. Like a nomad? Yes, just like a nomad. She would try for her own life, discover for herself, in vast, heat-struck lands free of fog, the truth at the pure heart of things.

India Stories

To my father

Hobart, a cold night, frosty, blue-black. Inside, a party. Seventies music, Deep Purple, King Crimson, red lights, blue lights alternating. People stood, lifted glasses, glanced over their shoulders. Sue was slumped in an armchair. She'd flown in from Perth the week before. A guy approached, eased down to her level. Introduced himself. Gordon. He was confident, friendly, wanted to talk. About what? Stories, he said, and handed her a glass of red.

'I was in India,' Sue started, 'travelling by train from Varanasi to Patna, noticed a bare patch on the wall in the carriage. A clean rectangle. I leaned across. It said, "Space measuring six inches by ten inches formerly occupied by a mirror now stolen".'

Gordon laughed, rocked back on his heels. Sue leaned back. Red light glared on threadbare carpet. Led Zeppelin played the 'Stairway to Heaven' and death was on her mind. Her father had died five days before.

The afternoon of her father's funeral the air was still, smoky; birds flittered between bare trees. Dawn colours remained in the sky, pale lemon, aqua. A stillborn day. At the funeral parlour, friends and family members were dressed in furs, woollens, leather. She'd worn her white Arran jumper, grey jeans, black boots. She hadn't thought to dress up, hadn't realised. Her father always said she was thoughtless. Inside, a thick green carpet muffled sounds. The polished wood of chairs and wall panels. Light from the frosted windows fell on the wooden coffin where her father rested. He was tucked under a sheet, no, a shroud. He'd died in hospital. They'd given him a pacemaker. Too old at eighty-four for a new part. He'd struggled so long with the old.

In infancy, tubercular stomach. At eight, he went out to work. He pushed around a little trolley doing odd jobs. Nothing earned meant nothing to eat. Adulthood was poverty too, the war, Depression, war again. That was the part he'd been handed and he'd played it with courage. With great heart.

The funeral cortège in the grainy grey day was a line of cars wreathed in mourning. A ceremony traditional, ephemeral. A one-off, like a story told, never repeated.

'Your drink.' Gordon handed the glass to Sue. He knelt, leaning against the armchair.

'I met a guy at a station,' Sue said. 'Delhi Central, waiting for the train to Simla. Pinstripes, umbrella, briefcase. We chatted. He opened his briefcase. On business? Indian Civil Service? No. He took out stamp and an ink-pad. Stamped the back of my hand. "BK Ray" the stamp said. "Formerly Vice President Congress Party Manipur State. Now Sacked".'

'Like the stamp on the wall,' Gordon said. 'Every loss accounted for, in life.'

'Five months more of the stamp, before he took the last part he was to play. As a holy man. A sadhu in a loincloth, a staff, poverty, prayers, wisdom perhaps.'

'Why was he sacked?' Gordon asked.

'Corruption, of course.'

At the cemetery, they walked up to the chapel from the car park. The scent of fennel drifted on the cold air. There were flowers. Wreaths and bouquets, congregations of blooms banked along the paths, ranked across the squares of lawn, spiking the chapel windows, spilling out onto the porch. A nurses' strike. There was no one to collect the blooms to take to hospitals to cheer the sick. Her father had hated flowers. Ripped intruders out of his vegetable garden. Banned them from the house. He distrusted their gaiety, rejected their inconsequence in a harsh world. And here they all were, for his funeral, brilliant against the red brick of the mausoleum, a gay paean to his passing.

She looked away, across a hillside of stone. Headstones, tombstones, monuments. A line of black cypress. Movement. A train unspooled across the landscape, carriage by carriage, a flicker of images, scene by scene.

When Sue had worked in Fremantle, she'd caught the train each morning. She'd stood by open doors, warm air gusting in, the smell of iron and cinders. She watched the passengers: Italian stonemasons going to Karakatta Cemetery, visitors to the hospitals in Subiaco, kids to a sheltered workshop somewhere. And once, her father with his beret, his red-checked work shirt, his Gladstone bag hanging open with his lunch, the thick belt he used as a strap lying loose on the floor. He sat with the stonemasons, cheerful, relaxed, not gaunt, reserved as he was usually. What was he doing here, where was he going? How could it be him? Had she imagined seeing him as he would've been if he'd lived here, in Perth with its ease and warmth? Is there an infinity of lives to choose from?

She had thought so when she was in India. Lives acted out on railway platforms, flickering scenes between arrivals and departures. Lives determined by the receding roar of engines, the regular rush of crowds from carriages. No seasons but sunlight through smoke, mists of steam. No sky but steel girdered arches. Time in timetables, clanging bells and Victorian railway clocks above ticket booths. Their lives, why not her own?

The crematorium. After the service, a conveyor belt slid the coffin between bunched curtains. Life's a stage, a Punch and Judy show. And backstage? The furnace. Her father had known. He'd disdained religion. As a shop steward, he'd fought for trade unionism, socialism, the rights of the working poor. Most of all, he'd believed in his family, wanting to leave them no rotting body, no headstone. Just the house he'd built for them, and a few memories of the songs he'd loved, 'Delilah' from *The Merry Widow*, 'Roses are Blooming in Picardy', 'Maggie…'

Black silhouettes, spiky hair, laughter – a crowd of art students burst in. The party was taking off. Sound pulsed past her. She pushed through to the open front door. A starred night sky, Mount Wellington/kunanyi a frosted hump. She leaned on the door jamb. Her father had been in India, First World War with the Light Horse. He was a kid then, younger than herself, eighteen perhaps, his first time away from home. But he'd never told her about those times. Never told her his India stories to tell and retell, as continuity to defeat the discontinuity of his death.

Aurora Australis

They stood around the car, mother, son, father. The night towered above them, black with icy stars. The car glittered with frost in street lights, their auras fuzzy. The lines of the footpath and kerb vanished into the darkness. Service poles jutted at right angles to the street, high tension wires stretched taut merging into the blackness. The boy noticed. Trapped.

Feet stamped, a hand jerked, bodies moved. 'Blast!' Fingers pinched at the cold lock on the door. 'Dora, you got the keys? I've gone and brought the wrong ones.'

The woman dived into a pocket and brought out the car keys. She reached them over. The boy watched. Shifted. The keys fell to the ground.

'Christ, can't you hand them over properly?'

'Sorry, Stan, I'm sorry.'

A snicker.

'Belt the livin' daylights outa you, I'm warnin' you.'

'Robby?' Dora tried to catch her son's eye.

He ignored her, slouched away, shoulders hunched against her. She sighed, her breath a freezing vapour around her face. A thump. Robby was kicking the tyres. She glanced at her husband, hands clenching with anxiety. But Stan had the car door open and was getting into the driver's seat. Dora relaxed. The engine was running before Stan reached across to unlock the passenger doors. She got in.

'Rob! What the hell are you playin' at, pissin' round out there!'

Dora tensed. He was in enough trouble at school, with his smoking and wagging it. He'd changed, that boy. Become surly, not the cheery little lad he used to be, loving nothing better than to walk to the shops with her, carrying the shopping back, just a few odds and ends, chatting the whole way… Was it just his age? Not drugs, anything but drugs.

'Here.' Stan tossed a rag to his son. 'Clean off the back window.'

Dora tucked a rug under her legs against the cold vinyl, and fastened her seatbelt. Her arms were warm in the pink mohair jumper she'd knitted, its collar pulled right up to her ears, her glasses on the end of her nose almost meeting it. Robby glanced at her as he handed back the cloth. His heart ached for her simple goodness, and he thumped his head in anger, trying to dispel the feeling. Dora tucked her arms into her sleeves and cautiously allowed her spirits to rise. It was Friday night, they were going up to her mother's, just to say hello, how're you keepin', then off to buy KFC and ginger beer, though Stan'd have his six-pack as usual, while they watched the footy on television. They never watched at her mother's. Dad was a soccer fan, wouldn't have that sissy game on his telly, he said. Though it was Mum's telly. Robby and Dora had saved for months to get it for them. Save them sitting around the fire bickering. *Charlie's Angels* Dad loved, him being a Charlie, of course.

The car cruised down the drive and onto the road. Dora rubbed a porthole in the passenger window and looked out. Empty streets, streetlights a halo of frosted silver, no one about. That was what she liked about the car. You could leave your problems behind and just sit there, cosy as anything, a happy family in their warm cocoon as the world sped by, empty and desolate.

Except Robby had said to her last time in the car, 'What's movin' Mum? We aren't movin', the landscape isn't movin'…'

'The car, we're in the car…'

'Yeah, sittin'. It's technology that's movin'.'

The things he came out with! Made you think.

'Minty, Robby?' She rattled the packet at him.

He took several. She unwrapped one for Stan and handed it stickily to him.

They were going through the shopping centre. 'Slow down, Stan, I want to look at the displays.'

White goods bathed in light, smart interiors, screens showing holiday ads of semi nude women cavorting on white beaches blue seas. She wasn't impressed, though Stan, she noted, could never keep his eyes off those ads. 'Look at those kitchens.'

'Pristine,' Robby said.

Pristine? Where did that boy get his words from? Dora eased the minty off her tooth with her tongue, choked, screamed, 'Stan!'

He braked and veered. 'What now?'

'We haven't turned off for the old way to Mum's!'

'Gawd's sake! Goin' up the freeway. Must be all of two ks longer the old way.' He could open the machine out on the freeway, no cops about tonight. 'I can open her out,' he said, 'give the engine a burst.'

'Real bad for the engine on a cold night,' Robby said. 'You'll fuck it.'

'Enough from you!' Stan aimed a blow at Robby in the back seat.

He ducked and snickered.

Dora sucked convulsively on her minty. They always went the old way. She knew it so well, remembering the times when she was a kid, growing up in the area. She still loved the bush, though so much had gone, taken by smart houses, newly built dream homes. She liked to think of herself living in one. The people in these houses, glimpsed around a table having dinner, or standing on their angled porches with a glass in their hands… She was as good as them, and she sniffed.

Stan turned onto the freeway, swung out from behind a van, tail light winking, and roared up the fast lane. A smooth surface rising out of the blackness, pierced by the headlights, devoured by the speed of his car, while all Dora saw was black asphalt sparkling with frost, hopefully no black frost around or they'd be done for.

Below them to the left, the lights of the city fell away just like, Robby thought, a distant galaxy, or a mother ship sinking out of sight around the shoulder of the hill. He rolled the minty papers into a ball and flicked it at his father's neck. Then started, just as they were turning onto the exit. What was that ahead in the sky?

'What's that, Robby?'

He was staring out of the side window, rubbing with his sleeve, then he opened the window.

'Fuckin' hell!' Stan said. What's goin' on?'

'There! In the sky… See, Mum?' She leaned sideways. 'Lights!'

'Close that window!'

No one took any notice.

'Like curtains, Mum.'

'Oh yes…' She could see nothing, but wanted to please Robby.

'It's getting brighter!'

'You mean…' and realised with a shock that she could see something. A green shimmer, deep in some parts, light in others, rippling like the folds of shantung silk, but vast, across a million miles, shooting across the sky, so fast!

'Look at that!' Robby gasped. He leaned on her shoulder, his face beside hers.

'Do you think it's maybe a…' He struggled for the words.

'Spaceship,' Stan guffawed. 'You're seeing the pictures before you've turned on the bloody set!' Veering into the left lane, foot on the accelerator.

Dora gazed absently, her jaw still, and the word popped into her head. 'Aurora!'

'Aurora,' Robby lingered over the word. He'd read about them when he was doing detention in the school library one lunchtime. 'Aurora Australis.'

The car cruised into the night, and, heads together, mother and son gazed at the iridescent curtains shimmering beyond any borders and boundaries, edges and wires.

'Something to do with sunspots,' Robby murmured. 'When there's a lot of sunspot activity, you get auroras, like, the earth's electromagnetic field.'

Dora gazed at him. 'Electro what?'

'Electro bullshit,' Stan said uncertainly. 'Close that fuckin' window.'

'Dad, stop the car, I want to see it better.'

'No way. You'll freeze to the asphalt on a night like this.'

'Stan,' Dora ordered, 'pull over.'

He jerked. Those glasses on her nose, the way they glinted. 'Gotta get to your mother's!' But he braked to a stop.

They got out, and stood there, like a pair of idiots. And he was the only one with any nous, stayin' out of the cold. Slowly they turned, their faces dark, the dumpy shape of his wife, the stringy length of his son outlined by street light, gazing upwards, and suddenly he was afraid. What if he lost them?

After a while, they got in the car and drove on, silent, ecstatic.

Arriving at the house, 'There's Mum!' Dora exclaimed. 'What's she doing out here?'

'Nan!' Robby leapt out of the car, followed by Dora and Stan. 'We saw an aurora!'

'Mum? What's wrong?'

'Well,' the old lady croaked, 'I'm waiting for the ambulance.'

'Ambulance? Stan, come on, Mum.' They helped the old lady inside.

'It's your father.'

'How is the old bugger?' Stan said.

'His breathing's real bad, Dora. He can hardly drag a breath into his lungs.'

'Shut the front door, Robby. Where is he, Mum?'

'Down the end bedroom, it's warmer there. I said it's warmer down the end bedroom, you'll be more comfortable, I said.'

Dora pushed open the bedroom door. 'Dad?'

He lay flat on the bed, his head straining forward on the pillow. The coverlet heaved with the rise and fall of his chest. 'Come to see a dead man,' he gasped.

'Oh, Dad…' She gathered herself together. 'They'll give you oxygen in the ambulance.'

'I'm not going anywhere in no ambulance,' he gasped.

'I said to him he'd be better off in the hospital. The doctor said his lungs are shot. I said, you'd be better off…'

'Too right, Charlie,' Stan interrupted her flow. 'Get you through the night. Right as rain tomorrow, eh Dora?'

'You'll be better tomorrow, in hospital.'

'Yes, Dora.' The old man gave in.

'The ambulance'll be here anytime now.'

'It's here!' Robby called out. 'The ambulance is here.'

'Charlie?' Dora's mother moved to the bedside to help him up.

Dora took her arm. 'It's all right, Mum, they'll take care of everything.'

'Mrs James?' A paramedic appeared. 'Your husband?'

'That's right…'

'Straight down here,' Stan said.

Another paramedic appeared with a stretcher. Dora's mother hovered.

'Poor old sod,' Stan said. 'She's goin' in with him?'

'I should think so.'

The paramedics emerged from the bedroom, carrying the old man on the stretcher. They manoeuvred it out to the ambulance, parked behind Stan's Holden. Robby ran along with them.

'Robby!'

'Don't shout at him,' Dora snapped at Stan. 'He's fond of his grandpop.'

'Just want him to check the house windows. Right, Robby? I'll do the lights and heater. Go out with your mum, Dornie.'

Dornie. How long since he'd called her that? She grabbed her mother's coat and scarf off a hook in the hall and went outside.

The back doors of the ambulance were open, its white interior lit up, blue curtains at the windows. The paramedics had angled the stretcher inside and lowered it onto a wide bench along one side. They were attaching a mask to the old man's face, linked to an oxygen bottle.

Dora helped her mother into her coat and wrapped the scarf, 'Where shall I sit, officer?' her mother asked the paramedic.

'In the back with Dad,' Dora urged, but the orderly slammed shut the doors.

'Up front with me, dear,' he said, as if it was special, just for her. George'll stay with your husband.'

Tears stung Dora's eyes at the sight, through the back window, of the old man straining beneath his oxygen mask. The engines roared, exhaust billowed as it backed up the drive.

Right here, where she was standing, had been the three-roomed shack they'd lived in for four years – four children, two adults – built out of fibro and the wooden crates that cars came in. Lying in bed, shivering under old coats on long winter nights, she'd read Queensbridge Motors stencilled on the boards, seen the stars through the gaps, the same stars, heard winds roaring down like freight trains, the same vast black nights as tonight. Her father had built the house, brick and tile, weekends. How had he done it? She'd never appreciated him trying so hard, wanting so much for his kids. And what had she done? Married the first bloke who'd come along. Stan.

'Mum?' Robby stood by her.

They watched until the red tail lights had turned and disappeared.

'Tell you what…' Stan joined them. 'We'll go home down the old way.'

What was he talking about? She stepped away from him, looked back, saw a husband, a son, the dark house. In the frosty night sky, the aurora had faded as surely as had her dreams. Well, it was time that changed.

'Come on, Robby.'

He opened the passenger door for her, for his mother. Shadows fell across their faces. They moved to the car, got in and, rear lights blinking red, they drove away.

Christmas at the Graces'

I was twelve years old when I went to stay at the Graces'. We lived at Dongara then, on the coast about forty miles south of Geraldton, where Dad was the headmaster of the local school. It was the Christmas holidays but Mum was ill and Dad had to drive her down to Perth for an operation. I was farmed out to the Graces for a few weeks.

Dad came in to my bedroom that morning, dressed in his good suit. 'Come on, Teddy!' He said. 'We've got to get going!'

I rolled out of bed and went into the kitchen, where Mum was sitting at the table, pale and quiet. My sister Annie was at the table, dressed in a new cotton frock and white socks and patent leather sandals, dressed to go down to Perth with Mum and Dad. She was quiet and pale too, but with excitement, stifled with it. I didn't envy her, though; I knew I would have a good time at the Graces'.

Mum pushed my bowl of porridge across, and she smiled. 'Now, you be a good boy while I'm away and give Grandma Grace a hand about the place.'

I nodded and that was all she said.

I went back to my room and pulled my clothes on. I didn't have any luggage because I'd taken it over to Grandma Grace the day before in the cart pulled by Jenny, my donkey. I heard Dad helping Mum out to the car, and I rushed outside. It was a long, hot trip to Perth. They had to leave early; it would take until nightfall to get there. We all squeezed into Dad's single-seater Chevrolet and drove over to Grandma Grace's.

Grandma Grace had a little stone cottage on the road between Dongara and its port, Port Denison. It sat there nicely in the rolling wattle scrub country, and as we drove up, Grandma Grace came out to meet us dressed in her old-fashioned blue dress, with a kind smile for my mother. She shooed me inside before I could even go round the back to give Jenny a pat. I looked back and all I saw of Mum was a flutter of her hand at the car window and Annie's big eyes staring out at me as they drove off.

My best mate was Roy Khan. He was half-Afghan and lived in Dongara with his mother. His father was dead and I don't know how his mother kept body and soul together. They didn't have much of a life in Dongara, the place was that narrow-minded. I couldn't see why people were so down on the Afghans. I remember them as tall, handsome men who kept to themselves. They did a good job of work taking a big Ford van round the properties of the wheat belt, stocked with goods, textiles, condiments, that sort of thing for sale. Roy took after his father, thin and dark, while I was stumpy and fair, like my English parents, thickset and dogged. We made a good pair, with Jenny and the cart.

Roy and I got around just the same while I was at Grandma Grace's. We'd get some gear together, a bit of tucker, a bit of chaff for Jenny, and off we'd go for three or four days at a time. We never went far, usually down to the beach at Port Denison, and we'd camp out, like drovers, we thought. In the evening, we'd light a little fire, cook some snaggers and boil the billy, while the sun sank through a fiery sky into the Indian Ocean. We'd wrap up in our blankets for the night and sleep like dead dogs, then we'd be up and about in the cool, piccaninny dawn. Roy and I spent hours and hours in the water, swimming, catching fish, diving for coral off the jetty, collecting shells off the reef; and we'd run up and down the beach, the sand burning our bare feet, making forts and moats; then we'd collect shells and seaweed and sea animals in our shirts, pore over them, swap them, have a fight over them, and the next day we'd tip them out and start all over again. When we ran out of food, we'd eat fish. Jenny liked a fish too. Then we'd head back to Grandma Grace's, our hair bleached and sticking to our heads with salt, burned almost black by the sun.

Two weeks before Christmas, Grandma Grace said it was time I stayed up at Sid, her son's place, in the wheat belt. He could do with a hand, she said. When Roy came round that morning, I told him I was going, and could he keep an eye on Jenny for me.

He gave me a long look. 'When's your ma comin back?' he asked.

'When she's better. Pretty soon, I reckon.'

Come to think of it, no one had said when exactly, but it had to be before the end of the school holidays.

Roy stared at me for a bit longer. 'My da,' he said finally, 'when he went away crook, he never come back.'

Cripes, well, that threw me. I hadn't even thought of Mum not coming back. But Daisy, Grandma Grace's daughter, was calling me, so I just said, 'See yer!' and left. But his words stuck with me.

Daisy drove me up to Three Springs in Sid's Oldsmobile, and that was a treat. Could Daisy drive! She was a pretty remarkable woman for her times, Daisy Grace. She could ride and shoot with the best of 'em, do any farm work about the place. She spent her evenings down at Dongara at the schoolhouse with us, listening to records, light classical, jazz, on our Salonola gramophone, and if we had any visitors, she'd dance. That's how we got to know the Graces, through Daisy.

Sid and his brother Dingo Doug lived on their property eight or ten miles beyond Three Springs. The property was big, sheep and wheat, but the place they lived in was a real dump. It was a small place, a few rooms and a veranda, set on capped stumps to keep the white ants out, made of vertical galvo with a pitched roof of galvo. It had a stunted wattle for shade, but all around was bare earth so hot it burned your feet. All else there was to the place was a shed for farm machinery and a big haystack, fodder for the horses. Up against the back of the house was a fence bordering a huge paddock of wattle and low gums. A flock of white cockatoos used to alight on a dead gum just beyond the fence. As always in the bush, it's hard, hot and rough, but there's always beauty too and for me it was those birds rising out of that tree and circling against the brilliant blue sky.

Well, the place was stinkin' hot and full of flies. Sid used to sit at the table of a morning, cup of tea in his hand, pestered by flies. He'd bang his hand on the table and there'd be a heap of dead flies. More flies would swarm there for a feed. He'd bang his hand down again, and that way he'd end up with a mountain of dead flies. Didn't seem to make any difference! Sid was an ex-jockey, small and wiry, a real tough agate. Work! Could he work.

Dingo Doug, his brother, he was the opposite. He was a big, solid bloke, but lazy! Did nothin' about the place. The way he earned his living was the same way he earned his nickname, by getting the dingo bounty, maybe five shillings a tail. He wore leather chaps and a gun belt with six guns, just like in the Wild West, and he used to run those dingoes down on horseback, firing off his six-shooters. His horse was a big chestnut called Garry. They were inseparable, a bit like me and Jenny. When Dingo Doug went drinking in the Three Springs Hotel, Garry would carry him back home and everyone reckoned he'd stagger from side to side to allow for Doug's drunken lurches in the saddle.

I went up to Three Springs to work, and work I did. There was plenty to do. Apart from the wheat which had to be bagged and sewn and taken into Three Springs, we had to mow what was left with the reaper and binder. It was bound into stooks and kept as fodder. There was a lot of pink-eye in the sheep, of which Sid had about three thousand. You could tell which sheep were affected because it blinded them, and they stumbled around the place and banged into things. Well, they had to be chased up for their eyes to be washed in a solution.

I tried to do everything that Sid did, even though I was only twelve. I even tried to lump those bags of wheat, 183 pounds they weighed, like he did. And then, I had this fear about Mum, and what if she never came back, like Roy Khan's dad? And in some way it was all connected with Dongara. I missed the place, even though I was only away for two weeks. Three Springs was nothin', just an arid wheat belt town on the Midland line, while Dongara was as pretty a place as you'd find with its fine stone buildings, the Moreton Bay figs in the main street and the

River Irwin flowing through. Not to mention Port Denison and the beaches. And Christmas was coming up and that was always a big time at our place. Mum always did the full thing with roast turkey, plum pudding, decorations, carol singing. A real English Christmas, she always said, with presents Dad made for us, even though the heat was always over the century.

Christmas Day arrived, stinkin' hot, and Sid and I drove in his Chevy truck into Three Springs, loaded up with bags of wheat. Sid drove to the railway siding and then he went straight across into the Three Springs Hotel. He stayed in there drinking and yarning all day, and I spent the whole day lumpin' those 183-pound bags. The sweat poured off me and the flies drove me silly. When I'd offloaded them, I turned round and shifted bags of super which we were taking back to the property, off the railway bogie and onto the platform, and this was an entirely different proposition. The bags were hard to handle; they were soft and floppy and the super got everywhere, in my hair and eyes and right through my clothes, though I had only shorts on. By the time I'd finished, I'd had it and Sid staggered out of the pub and across the road.

'Good lad,' he said. 'You've worked your arse off!' Then he took me over to the pub to shout me a beer, my first alcoholic drink.

We were just crossing the veranda when Sid's Oldsmobile came haring down the street with Daisy Grace at the wheel. She must've known Sid would be in the pub, because she skidded to a stop. When the dust had settled, I saw Dad was in the car, and Annie too, bouncing on the back seat. But no Mum! I must've gone as pale as a sheet because Dad was out of the car like a cut cat.

'It's all right, Teddy.' He grabbed me. 'Your mum's back home at Dongara. I didn't want to bring her out in this heat.' He shook me by the shoulders gently and Annie pushed a packet into my hands, my Christmas present.

I opened it, and it was the most beautiful set of leather harness for Jenny, and my dad had made it for me. I almost blubbered, but Sid handed me a glass of beer.

'Here's to the worker!' he said. 'Happy Christmas!'

We drove back to the property to collect my gear. I said goodbye to Dingo Doug and Garry, and then it was back home to Dongara for Christmas. Back to Mum and Grandma Grace and Christmas dinner cooked by Daisy, to Jenny and her new harness, and to one in the eye for my mate Roy Khan. I was that pleased!

At the Creek

'Okay, fellas, settle down, there's work to be done. Sit down!'

And we jump to it! No way we can give Banjo hell after what happened yesterday. Grade 10 level 1–2 English, Lowton Boys High, why shouldn't we give it to her? English teachers are a pushover, soft do-gooders, break their necks to be understanding. Especially when we come in Monday morning wasted after a weekend on the grog. Not that Banjo took that from us.

'Take the consequences!' she shouts and kicks us out of the quiet reading area where we're trying to sleep it off, and it's stiff shit whether you're Animal or Gay. Bad!

But she's not as bad as maths/science: look sideways and it's out with the cane, 'specially the Senior Masters. Macho-sadists Kinghit calls them and I dunno whether it's because he's dumb or bright.

The class is quiet, waiting for the shit to hit the fan.

I'll fill you in. Kinghit is the boss of the Animals and me, Shane, I keep the Gays in order and that's how the class divides up except for a few rejects, like Daniel, who's soft in the head, and Garco and Slops, they're sort of sub-Animals, know what I mean?

The Animals, they're slag! Wear muscle shirts and earrings, tattooed biceps and are level one Terminals. Not like us, the Gays. We're smart level 2s, neat hair and school uniform, follow cool music, rap, Sting and hey! I found this Cat Stevens tape, made a comeback, Banjo said. She let me play it in double English and she goes all soft and dreamy, said she used to play 'Tea for the Tillerman' before, before… She goes off in a dream and I pass a smoke under the desk to Yoplait, and the Rat intercepts. I kneecap him, Kinghit slags on Daniel and all hell breaks out. Banjo finds Garco's ripped the barcode off the cassette player (yep, tapes – we're a poor state school), and the whole lot goes back to the library.

You think we're wild? The Animals are the worst, but I've seen Banjo drag Kinghit off a desktop when he's been laying into Garco and Slops with a chair, and Kinghit, he's big! Solid, and blond with it. She's soft on him, no kiddin'. He copies the lyrics off heavy metal numbers and she's rapt! Thinks he's a poet! He got kicked out of a Catholic college for Satan worship, he says, and flexes his Prince of Darkness tatt to Banna and Willy the Porn, and sneers at Jesus, the Virgin Preacher, virgin, like Daniel. Banjo just laughs and says to get it all down on paper, but we're into chords, not letters. Hold it! Scott Lacey has just come in with a message for Banjo; she's going out five minutes and we're to be absolutely silent. Shit, a reprieve! While she's gone, I'll tell you about yesterday.

Double English, end of term, getting slack. So we conned Banjo into letting us play cricket on the oval over at the creek, one of the school's boundaries. S'funny, but over there, right at the jagged edge of factories, houses, junk yards, beyond the willows, the school sort of shrinks, its buildings look puny. Maybe it's the Mountain, it looks so much bigger, frowning over the suburbs, mist and cloud dissolving streaked with rainbows, storm showers marauding, like it's real and we're fake… Anyway, we got a couple of bats, set up the wickets, got a ball out of the sports store and skived over to the oval. Two teams, Animals v. Gays of course.

'Like life,' Banjo says, and grins at me.

Animals won the toss. Went in to bat, jeering, and I had a feeling something was on, dunno why. It was quiet at first, playing the game. Banjo's fielding for us, not leaning on the boundary fence in high heels, arms crossed over her boobs, bored stiff like most women teachers. She ripped off her shoes and jacket and was into it. 'Strip!' Yoplait and Dipstick yell, but she shot the ball at Yoplait, he dropped it and the laugh was on him. Then Kinghit whacked a beauty to the boundary. I sent the Rat to get it, we're all looking for a return, then this racket breaks out.

'The Animals, 'Garco and Slops,' they yell, 'smokin'!'

Banjo hares over to the nets, where they were sitting out the game and, sure enough, smoke is wisping up. I race over there too, and Garco's writhing on the ground howling and holding his ear and Slops is laughing fit to piss himself. 'She stuffed it in his ear!'

And Banjo's raging, 'You worms!'

Suddenly, there's this shriek, no kidding, chilling enough to freeze-dry your heart. We spin around. Over at the creek the Animals have got Daniel strung up in the willow, stripped down to his underdaks, his little white legs dangling. No one's on the pitch, I notice, as we hurtle across the oval. They're all with Kinghit, getting a nice little red hot burn going under Daniel.

'King!' Banjo screeches and Kinghit jerks around, mouthing 'Fuckin' hell.' He thought Banjo'd be with Slops and Garco up at the office, instead it's him and the Animals caught like rats in a trap.

There's a scuffling as they try to kick out the fire and there's this almighty crack and rip, and the branch holding Daniel, arms outstretched as Banna and Willy the Porn try to haul him down, breaks and half the willow comes crashing down, Daniel, Banna and Willy the Porn riding the lot.

'Whooeee!' Banna yells, and Daniel lands smack on Kinghit in a storm of fronds and embers. The bough bounces, bodies fly, Kinghit is flattened.

'For Christ's sake,' Banjo yells, as she heaves Daniel out of the wreckage.

No one was hurt but it took us the rest of the double to clean up the mess. Dragging the broken willow down to the creek and making sure the fire was dead, ash cleared away. She made Kinghit find Daniel's clothes and help him get himself together. Banjo was furious with us all, not just the Animals: we all let it happen, didn't we? We all forced her into punishing Kinghit, marching him up to the office, didn't we?

'Boys!' Banjo's back, looking real ugly. Uh oh, she got it in the neck at the office. She looks us over, eyes angry. 'Reports!' she says. We stiffen. 'References.' We're hanging out for good ones, how else will we get jobs when we leave? 'As far as I'm concerned,' she pauses, looks over us, hating our guts, 'you wrote them for yourselves, yesterday.'

Hey! There's groaning in the air, dirty looks, despair and why am I in the shit? Had nothing to do with it. And Daniel? What about him?

'Collective responsibility,' she says as if she's reading my mind. 'You all were there. Consequences!'

'And you!' I shout.

And she whips around, shocked, and I battle her with my eyes, forcing her back, the whole class tense.

Then her eyes drop, her face eases. 'I have,' she says quietly, and suddenly we're all scared.

Maybe she's got the sack, lost her job and it's our fault. She looks away. Kinghit's at the door, holding his shoulders square, bulk tight like always, but hey! His hair's smart, he's in school uniform! He gives Banjo a real look, half ashamed, but grinning and she looks back, doesn't say a word. Suddenly I can see why Banjo's soft on him: she's not just an English teacher, she's a woman, more, a person, and he sees it. He walks to his desk with his usual tough roll, sits, looks at her and when she turns to us she's almost back to normal.

'You've got two weeks,' she says. We know she means our reports and stuff. 'I want all the work you've started and not finished, forgotten, torn up or lost, completed.'

Silence. We'll fudge it somehow.

'This double, for those up to scratch, I want you to start your last piece of work, get it to first draft for now.' She walks to the windows. 'A poem, short piece, story, script, and the theme is crossing a boundary…from the past to the future, from school into the world, from the everyday into nightmare.'

Daniel squints his dark eyes and I'm shocked, they're so bright.

'From captivity into freedom.'

We're quiet, ruling up, straightening pages, thinking.

'Choose your boundary: a seashore where land meets water, a wall dividing two places, a mountain range, a creek…'

Yoplait is already writing, Dipstick's gazing out at the sky, Kinghit's staring at Daniel, looking real puzzled.

'Borders and boundaries,' Banjo goes on, 'are where it's at. Love, death, revenge… Things, people can get ugly, then change into the new and beautiful.'

I know what's she's saying. I title my story 'At the Creek', and it starts, 'Soft, innocent, fragile whiteness of skin transparent to veins and bones, he's a living breathing sacrifice and we all see it, assembled in the shadows at the Creek. And I wonder what it is that I, Kinghit, want to drag and tear from his weakness to make my own…'

A History of Roses

To my mother

Jane stands in the kitchen. Strong, straight, head thrown back. She's just come back from the Douglas Parker Rehabilitation Centre. Not that she's sick or incapacitated. No, it's a day out each Thursday, a cheap lunch, a chat, and anything might happen! Today, it's a story about a lizard she rescued from the fruit and veg stall in the mall, bringing it home in a paper bag to set free in her garden. Last year, at her eightieth birthday in a large Greek restaurant in the city, she'd astonished the family by winning the belly dancing competition. Bored with family gossip, she'd wandered into the front room where I'd seen her as I was going through to the wash room, swaying exotically in a circle of women. She'd returned to the family table, clapping her hands with delight. I won the belly dancing competition. They said the winner is…Janie!

Now she stands in the kitchen, getting me a cup of tea. On the radio, a deep voice with a northern English accent says Roses, we all love 'em. Let's talk about roses. Jane smiles, leans on the bench and listens.

Alba roses, gallea roses, bourbon roses. Peace, sunshine, the fresh air, the countryside. That is what roses mean to Jane. Born in the slums, christened Janie – scullery maids were always called Janie, they thought they'd save themselves the bother, she said. His father worked on the barrows, down the North End Road, spending his time with his horses in the mews. And Jane? Too intelligent. She was the first of her family to read, and with few children's books, she read to her father Dickens, Chekhov, Tolstoy. She collected books off the stalls and set up a library in the street. At thirteen she was admitted to an advanced school for girls, where she was addressed as Miss Powell. She started learning languages, horticulture, business studies, until her father took her away. He sent her down the North End Road lugging bags of potatoes, selling vegetables. Work which had already killed her sister.

At that point, Jane could see no future. The present is the bitter cold, the early morning dark, the cries and curses of the costermongers. Despairing, she imagines a different reality. An English country cottage overhung with roses. A place so far from her present reality it might as well be on another planet.

Jane is a young woman now, married to Charlie. She has her first child, a boy, my brother Harry. She lives in the mews above the stables, in one room. No heat, no light, no running water and the stink of horse ordure. Jane clings all the more to her dream; it is all she has to lighten the darkness.

Eventually, the family moves to a housing estate. Clean air, much more space, and Jane settles down. She is happy, accepts the present, can face the future, but dreams are not so easy to kill off. They send her secret subversive messages. The street names: Old Farm Road, Cuckoo Hill, Court Mead. Look at her beautiful garden, blooming behind the privet hedge. Pax rose, drooping with masses of creamy white blooms. Prosperity, showers of white; peace and prosperity lie in the present, the roses tell her. And Jane believes them.

Nineteen fifty-five Australia. Bushfires, bull ants, blowflies. Under the gum trees, a shack. No bathroom, no toilet, no garden. Buffeted by wind, clouds, storms, silence. A landscape dominated by a blue-black mountain snowy in winter. A great fall of air to a chastened little town clinging round a harbour. A landscape of dream, but to Jane, a nightmare through which she moves wrapped in her memories.

While Jane had invented an idyll set in a romantic past, Charlie had seen his paradise lying in the future. He would escape war, defeat poverty, deny class. Turning his back on Europe, he would live his own life, buy his own land, build his own house. And so he did.

But dreams, like the past, like roses, are tenacious. Look at the house that Charlie built. Note the steeply pitched roof dappled with moss, the dormers, the big square chimney, the wide eaves where swallows dive in and out, so like an English country cottage in a hundred villages. Jane responds to the cues, plants roses. Cuttings from English roses brought to Australia since settlement, handed down the generations. Under the bedroom windows, a tea rose of tender pink blooms, Duchess de Brabant, often found flowering against pickers' huts and shepherds' cottages. Against a scree of boulders excavated from the house foundations, a tea rose of full creamy flowers shaded with ruby, first grown against settlers' cottages. On the northern wall, she grows white roses, Niphetos, often found thriving in colonial gardens. And an Alba, Madam Plantier, with clusters of double white blooms which thrives in old cemeteries, memorial gardens and parks. Heady, fragrant, romantic.

Two weeks ago, Jane went with Ethel and other friends from Douglas Parker, to the town hall to an exhibition of historic photographs. Unfortunately, they caught the lift down instead of up and found themselves wandering along dark corridors. Back at the lift, the doors opened and out stepped a fine old gentleman, as Jane describes him to me. Tall, straight with a snowy head of hair. They chatted. He came from Wales, he said. Prove it, the women said. Sing us a song. Sing us 'The Roses are Blooming in Picardy'. So he did, and Jane joined in. Their sweet old voices mingled and twined together, climbing up through Rates and Engineering, rambling through Building and Planning, tangling in the Lord Mayor's chambers, finally blooming over the town from the top storey of the town hall.

In the kitchen, Jane opens her mail. She's received a birthday card, for tomorrow she turns eighty-one. On the front of the card is a picture: a thatched cottage is basking in the sun, roses twining around the door, a swallow holding a sign saying Happy Birthday. At eighty-one her dream is still alive, of her cottage in the country.

The Artist

Why did he ask me to do it? I'm only seventeen, and he's an old man of forty; shit, maybe, even more. He didn't have the right, officer… It was cool here, before he showed.

'Write your statement,' he says. 'Sign at the bottom.' Pokes his finger.

He's an artist, so what! I seen him do dumb everyday things like putting out the garbage, buying milk at the shop, papers. What's so special, shouldn't he be crazy, throw wild parties, wear weird gear, have two women and get drunk if he's an artist? Nah. You never see anyone at his place.

'His residence is…'

'A shack on the cliff above the water. Number 1. Told you.' Great for a real cool scene, just get rid of the mess, and you're cruisin'. Sick sound system, crazy lighting and you're ready to rap! He says the view's enough across the water. So? We don't go all spaz because of a view, do we?

At home, we're straight dudes. Two-storey place with a fancy balustrade and a media room, two cars, spa… Dad commutes to town; he's a sales manager, automobiles, even works back nights. Mum's a nurse, works shifts at the hospital earning extra so's she can give us kids everything, me Sharon and my bro Shane. We look good, got the right gear, leisure activities, music…

'When did you first meet Mister Jones?'

'Who?'

'The victim.'

'At the pharmacy.' He comes tottering in. Greasy hair, poor skin tone, daggy trousers and some sort of hairy jumper with leather patches…in summer? He wants toothpaste, and I say, 'What brand, sir?' and he says 'Kolynos,' and I say, 'Is that Greek, sir?' Sylvie my boss says, 'Sorry, sir, that brand was discontinued in the seventies.' The seventies! You mean he hasn't cleaned his teeth since last century? Gross! Sylvie takes his prescriptions while I sort out the toothpaste, but he can't make up his mind! I shunt him over to the display, his crutches clattering, show him the range: Sensodyne Complete Care, Cedel Sensitive, Colgate Total, Colgate Fluoride, Colgate Triple Action, Colgate Total Shield, Colgate Optic White, same toothpaste, different names, I know this, being in the profession. In the end he chooses Colgate Fluoride Free just as Sylvie brings back his prescription pills. I'm taking his card when he asks me if I'll help out with the house cleaning. I was shit surprised! I jumped back, hit the hats and sunnies carousel, they went everywhere and Sylvie was down on me. He offered me forty bucks an hour, how could I say no?

Next day, Thursday 3rd, officer, I go up there to the shack on the cliff. The door's open, I tap on it, call out, 'Hello, it's Sharon!' Nothing, so I tiptoe in. Oh my god, the mess. Stuff everywhere! A wall of books, more books stacked on the floor, can't even see the floor. Art magazines, bits of wood, paints, pictures leaning against the wall, a table covered in tins, tubes, splattered with paint, chairs fallen over… and weird things, a stuffed elephant with a cat riding it, a real cat, ginger, curled up…bottom half of a car, wheels and everything, like, under the table… I'm so busy looking around I don't even notice him.

He moves away from the window, leaning on one crutch. 'Thank you so much for coming, Sharon,' he says. Polite, I give him that.

'Not a problem!'

'I'm Max,' he says.

'Hi, Max.' He's got everything ready: broom, dustpan, vacuum cleaner, bucket and mop, dusting cloths, sponges, spray and wipe, and I'm into it, thinking, could drag this out two hours, eighty bucks, cash in hand, he'd better not ask me to do the loo.

'Cup of tea? Coffee?'

I'm here for work, so I say thanks, but no thanks.

Anyway, I'm going for it, with him saying now and then, 'Don't touch that,' and 'Leave that, I'll fix it later,' in such a quiet way I don't mind at all. No one talks to me nice like that at home, 'cept Mum, and she's hardly there, with work.

Then I notice he's drawing. Me? My hair up in a knot, scarf dangling, jeans split at the knees, old T-shirt, no make-up? Nah, must be the view he's getting down on paper. He swings on his crutches to another area – studio, he says. Do I have ta clean that? No, *forboten* or something he says, real quick. Half hour later, he comes out, offers me a cool drink but I'm finished, give him a little wave, make a time to come back and head outa there, forty bucks clear in my jeans pocket. Wicked!

Shane, my bro the in-house psycho, telling you, we don't need a reality show, we are it! Sorry, officer, I'm still writing. Anyway, he's watching midday TV and flicking though mags when I get in. Wonder he isn't gaming, that's the other dumb activity he feeds to his tiny brain cells. He's aggro as usual. I ignore him, I need a shower.

He follows me. 'I seen ya,' grabs my hair. 'Up at that dirty pervert's place. S'goin on?'

'Fuck off, ya gorilla!' And I knee him one.

'Fuckin bitch!' He shoves, I shove back. 'Got me those sufedrin, bitch?'

'No way, stealin' from Sylvie? Fuck you!'

'You don't, I will!'

Then the car's in the garage, Mum's home, getting the shopping out of the car, and I rush down to help.

Max's place next time, same but different. After I've washed the egg-smeary plates, coffee-crusted mugs, washed and put away knives and forks, mopped the floor, he says to stop for a cuppa. This time I say cool, keep doing a bit of tidying while he totters about with the jug of water. I take a look at art books he's got lying on the table. They mean nothing to me, but boy, they look crazy!

While the jug's on the go, he's leaning by the window, looking out.

'Lotta books you got,' I say.

'None of them beat the view.'

I stand by him. Seabirds wheeling, bay rising to hills and mountains like paper cut-outs, sky and water shades of blue, a line of yachts heading out, like origami boats. I go all dreamy, sorta get lost in it, don't notice him grabbing at me, handing over a sheet of paper.

'Here…'

'What's this, Max?'

'For you.'

It's me in my cleaning gear… Shit! I'm looking like another person, not boring Sharon working hours at the pharmacy, house-cleaning on the side. Can't tell you. It means heaps to me.

'Oh thanks, Max.'

Then the jug's boiling and he lurches to get it, crashes into a chair and I rush over to help.

We sit at the long table. I make a pass at clearing a space and finally he gets mugs of tea on the table and a poor little plate of dry biscuits. Honestly, you gotta feel sorry for him. He wants to know about my college course. Who wants to talk about school? Why do people think it's so shit fascinating? Can't wait to get clear, earning my own money and this forty bucks an hour is gonna get me there.

'Like, general studies, intro to psych, like, art, like hairdressing…' I can be polite when I want to.

'Art?'

'An elective, is all.'

'You should do more.'

'Why? No way that's gonna get me a job.'

'A job isn't everything.'

He's reading my mind? Anyway, that was it, no more questions. But I had some. Like, what happened to his legs? I can't help looking at them.

'MS,' he says, reading my mind.

What's that?

'Had it twenty years now.'

I try to think, has Mum ever mentioned MS?

'Multiple sclerosis.'

It sure sounds serious. 'So sorry,' I say. 'Will it…' Get better? Fix itself? What were the right words?

'It's my life now.'

His life? If it was my life, I'd top myself. 'But Max!'

'Sharon, life is life, you don't choose it.'

Uh oh, he's wrong there. I fully intend choosing my life.

He twists on his chair, looking around the room and I get it.

'You mean this?'

'S'right, Sharon.' He kinda shakes, takes a deep breath, acting like nothing's wrong, but no way he fools me, he's real bad.

I put out a hand. 'Hey hey! My Mum's a nurse. I'll get her up here, no problem.' I meant it, sure I meant it, but I never got the chance.

Home. Shane's in the garage, polishing the chrome on the Yamaha Mum and Dad got him for Christmas.

'Where've you been?' He fronts me.

'I'm late for the pharmacy.'

He grabs my hair, yanks me.

'Gotta get ready, Shane, let me go!'

'Mum'd sure like to know what you've been up to, like, who's been up ya.'

'Fuck off. I'll tell Dad!'

'When? Like when he's finished screwin' his ho, nights.'

My dad? 'Liar. He's working back five nights a week. For us.'

He laughs. 'I been checkin' on him. What's he gonna do when I tell him that old guy touched you up?'

'Fuck off, Shane!'

'That cripple, where'd he feel you up, c'mon…'

I jerk away from him.

'You get me the gear from the pharmacy, else I'm spillin' to Dad and Mum.'

I run upstairs, throw off my clothes and lock myself in the shower, turn it on full blast. Takes me forever to get clean.

Dinner time.

'Mum, where's Dad?'

She gets up, takes the plates to the dishwasher. I watch her. She stiffens, and I know…know what? She's bent over, so bony, so thin. And suddenly I'm worried. For her, not for Dad.

'Working back,' she says eventually.

Shane gives a rude sign with his finger. I smack down a glass.

Mum looks over. 'Dessert anyone?'

It's jelly and ice cream, like, we're little kids still.

Shane gives Mum this cute smile. 'Sharon's got a new job,' he says.

I could kill him. 'Only one hour a week, Mum.'

'I said to cut down your hours, Sharon.' She plonks down the bowls. 'College is more important.'

Shane wolfs his, red jelly spilling down his chin.

'Mum, it's a carer's job…' Making it up as I go. 'He's an old guy, got MS.'

But Mum's gone all vague, like she does sometimes.

Then Shane says, 'Sharon and me are goin' for a walk, hey, sis?'

Mum smiles. 'That's nice.'

'Down to the beach.'

The creep! I stay right there. Shane shoves back his chair. Gets out his phone. Taps away. He holds it up, showing a shot of the bikie gang he hangs out with. Dense Metal. Bunch of spotty creeps in fake leathers made in China. Dense all right. I hate them.

'I gotta give Mum a hand.'

He slouches out.

I try to talk some more about Dad. 'Does he really need to do overtime, Mum?'

'He's a manager, he has responsibilities.' She bends over to pick up a knife from the floor. Wipes it carefully.

My phone dings, a text from Shane. He's down in the garage. Get your ass down here, or we're gonna fire up that pervert's place. I crash the plates into the dishwasher and head downstairs.

Down in the garage. 'You haven't got the guts.'

He's swaggering around, waves his phone. 'Get the tribe onto the old creep, you want that?'

I hesitate. Shoulda gone straight upstairs to Mum. And what? Worry her even more? While Shane does something really stupid, and what about Max? If only Dad would come home right now and fix all this.

'The pharmacy.' Hands over a bike helmet.

'Pharmacy!'

'You're comin' or else…'

'Back window,' I blurt. I know it's shut real tight.

'Better be right, slut.' He shoves me.

I fall, grab a spanner lying on the concrete, bash his knee as grabs at me.

'Bitch! Shit, I'm fuckin' damaged, you ho!' He hobbles off.

I roll free and I'm outa there, hurtling up the road to Max's place, the roar of the Yamaha starting up way behind me. I burst in, slam shut the door.

Max is standing at the window, glass in his hand. So calm. He turns around. 'Sharon?' He puts his arm around my shoulders. 'What is it?'

What can I tell him, that my psycho brother's prowling outside, off his brain, calling in his dreck bikie mates?

'My psycho brother's outside, off his brain…'

'Like a drink?' Max helps me to a chair. All this fuckin' calmness, how's it gonna help?

'Max… He's out of control. Telling you!'

'I see.' As if he's used to this sorta drama. 'Sharon, what can he do that's…?' Worse than this, he meant.

I swallowed. 'He made me…'

'Do what?'

'Doesn't matter.'

I think of Shane, maybe he's breaking into the pharmacy as we speak. It's only glass. Was that a decision I made, telling him about it, or his for breaking in?

'Don't think about him.' He strokes my shoulder.

I rest my head on his chest. The smell of turps, paint, tobacco is so calming. Could this be my life? Doing something I believe in? Would that protect me, support me, give it meaning? If Max can do it with his wrecked body…

The door crashes. Shane bursts in, raging. 'Fuckin bitch! Window's barred!'

'Ha ha,' I sneer.

'Got in anyway.'

'You did what?'

'Sort you out,' he yelled. 'And you, dirty fuckin' pervert!' He throws a punch, misses, hits the table, everything goes clattering and crashing.

Max just stands there, wobbling, watching the chaos. I throw myself on Shane. He drags me down. Max staggers forward. Shane kicks out. Max falls, hits his head on the table edge. Blood.

'You bastard, hit a sick man!' I grab something off the table. Bash Shane. He falls, pill packets going everywhere and he's out to it. I stagger up, wrap a tea towel around Max's head. Get through on triple 0 to the police. 'Emergency! Shack on the cliff, number one!'

Why did Max pick on me for help? What help am I? All I did was bring trouble into his life.

I write my name, the bottom of the page.

The officer takes it. Reads it, like, so slow. What, is he dyslexic?

'Well?'

'The gentleman is not pressing charges.'

'What?' I drop the pen. 'So why am I making this statement?' I jump up to go.

'Just sit back down. There's the matter of the pharmacy break-in. Your brother's been interviewed. He's made a statement.'

'I'm saying nuthin'!'

'We'll see about that, miss.'

'My dad'll get me a lawyer, officer. Where's Mum? I'm outa here! Tellin' you!'

'Sit down!'

I calm down, like Max would want me to, and sit at that desk. But in my head I'm outa that place whatever happens, exiting Shane, Dad, the whole screwball mess of my family. All they done is try to lock me into their way. Hopeless. I know what I want, Max's shown me, and I aim to get it.

The Moths of War

It happened a few months after the death of my partner, George. I was – still am – devastated. Such an exceptional man, considerate, hospitable, an entrepreneur… Large, in all senses of the word. Loved nothing better than to have friends and associates for dinner, cooking a beautiful meal, glass of wine in his hand, holding forth while music played, opera, what else? Candles, an open fire in winter, in summer out at the table under the heritage trees… Perry, he'd say, let's live it up tonight. We'd dress for dinner, he'd cook, get out the vintage reds… Life was so very special, I miss it. This jacket I'm wearing, where is it? Givenchy, you know, perfect. George bought it for me for my fiftieth, in Rome, our last trip together. Italy, France, a cruise through the Mediterranean, Sicily, Venice…magnificent!

We shared a good life… But…there's always a but, don't you agree? George's was rather a large but. His books. You couldn't touch them. Reasonable, you might think? Every well rounded man should have a library. These days?

I call my wardrobe my library; every item is quality, and can tell a story. George used to complain. He wanted the wardrobe space for more bookshelves. I could handle the odd bookcase, antique preferably, as a complement to my tasteful interiors, but wall to wall in every room? How many, I asked George when we first met. A few thousand. A few thousand? More like twenty thousand!

He got them on the shelves before I even arrived – yes, he had his priorities. The hall, two living rooms, four bedrooms, the pantry, the kitchen, no room was spared the presence of books.

I loved, I still love, George, of course! So I took a deep breath and prepared to sail into a lifetime exploring the oceans, gulfs and bays of knowledge together in our tastefully restored Georgian country mansion… At Lower Marshes? Ever seen a more morose and desolate landscape?

Yes, George read, staying up to the small hours, no sign of dementia or Alzheimer's, early onset or late, his mind protected, no doubt, by his eccentricity. I could ask him anything, and he'd have an answer. I could request a book on a particular subject, off he would dash to find several references. You don't believe me? For example, he had fifteen books on military tanks, from World Wars I and II, not that I have the slightest interest in military ware; my tastes are lighter, I love American musicals, 'I'm singing in the rain…'

He died suddenly of a heart attack after doing his duty by a bottle of whisky late one night. I found him, slumped off his chair, fallen against a bookcase, his book still open.

I was in grief, as you can imagine. I wandered these rooms, remembering our good times, our best times, for weeks. Then I just had to get away from Lower Marshes for good. I called in the book-shop owners from the city. They were keen to buy, hell yes. Grabbing anthropology, archaeology, ecology and ancient history, rummaging through the Dark Ages to the Middle Ages, and on to the Tudors and later monarchies, salivating over his Chinese, Japanese and Indian collections, grabbing armfuls of books from walls of fantasy, science fiction, mystery novels.

Gleeful booksellers' cars and vans were parked outside, like the start of a funeral cortège without the flowers or the Funeral March. I waved them goodbye and deposited the cash in my account, already planning another trip to the Mediterranean on my own. Where I would stay, the cafés and the restaurants and the fashion houses. And then it happened.

I was checking the last room, the war room, which the booksellers weren't interested in but had George's favourites – tomes on the wars and revolutions of Europe, the Napoleonic campaigns, the Boer War, First World War, Second World War, China, Indochina – and it was almost impossible to move past military magazines stacked high on the floor, so I decided to take action. Taking an armful of magazines, I dumped them outside in a heap, piled brushwood on them and set them alight. Oh, the relief! Why stop there? I dashed back inside, was reaching for a volume of Winston Churchill's *History of the Second World War*, when something hit my face.

I looked around, nothing. I reached again for a book, and thunk! There's a moth lying on the floor feebly moving its legs. Weird. Then something was crawling on my neck, slap, another moth. Ugh! What's going on? I looked around the room. Nothing. The single guest bed was stripped to the mattress, the bedside drawers empty, the desk cleared… I listened. A faint hum, mmmm, the fridge? This wasn't the kitchen. So I took volumes one and two of Winston Churchill, and stacked them on the mattress, followed by volumes three and four.

A sudden whirring, a flurry, the room darkened as a whirlwind of moths spun out from the bookcase, filling the room! I hit out, flailing, but more and more whirled around my head, wings battering me, little claws scratching my face, the air filled with this ghastly humming rustling flittering. I wrapped my arms around my head and ran into the hall, the humming got louder, like a 747 taking off! A crash from the room. I dashed back. Books were falling off. A whole shelf toppled, releasing battalions of moths. I dived down the hall, A stream of moths was pursuing me, moths crushed underfoot as I ran, slamming doors behind me, screaming!

This is my retreat, this little room. The white walls glare, the light splinters. I must get away from here, they say. Overseas. But I'm safe here, the doctors, the medications. Sssh, can you hear the humming, it's there beyond the door, always there…tiny claws scratching, wings battering the windows… George! I'm sorry! Leave me alone! George!

Published Work

'The Dress', *The Tasmanian Review*, 1980

'Killing the Drake', *Hecate*, 1980

'Aurora, Australis', *Hecate*, 1984

'A Sense of Place' (rewritten as 'Refuge'), *Island*, 1984

'Exploration of Fog' (rewritten as 'i'), *Mattoid*, 1985

'Christmas at the Graces', *National Times*, 1985

'At the Creek Island', anthologised in *First Rights: the best of Island's first ten years*, 1987

'Bethlehem in Sydney', *Island*, 1989

'India Stories', *Preludes*, 1989

'Palmyra', *Island*, 1993

'Paradise Lost', *Island*, 1994

'Cull Island', *Island*, 1995

'Sisters', *Island*, 1997

'The Advertiser', *Picador New Fiction*, 1998

'State of the Heart', anthologised in *The Sky Falls Down: an anthology of loss*, Ginnindera Press, 2019

9 781760 417604